T0129235

The Adventures of
**Crawley McPherson,
Bug Man**

The Adventures of
Crawley McPherson, Bug Man

Jerome Goddard, Ph.D.

Illustrated by Leo Michael

THE ADVENTURES OF CRAWLEY MCPHERSON, BUG MAN

iUniverse books may be ordered through booksellers or by contacting:

iUniverse
1663 Liberty Drive
Bloomington, IN 47403
www.iuniverse.com
1-800-Authors (1-800-288-4677)

Because of the dynamic nature of the Internet, any web addresses or links contained in this book may have changed since publication and may no longer be valid. The views expressed in this work are solely those of the author and do not necessarily reflect the views of the publisher, and the publisher hereby disclaims any responsibility for them.

Any people depicted in stock imagery provided by Getty Images are models, and such images are being used for illustrative purposes only. Certain stock imagery © Getty Images.

Author Photo: Mississippi State University Extension Service photo. Used with permission.

ISBN: 978-1-5320-7985-6 (sc)
ISBN: 978-1-5320-7986-3 (e)

Library of Congress Control Number: 2019911249

Print information available on the last page.

iUniverse rev. date: 08/08/2019

AUTHOR'S NOTE

"The Adventures of Crawley McPherson, Bug Man" – is a work of fiction. Crawley McPherson and all other characters in this book are products of the author's imagination or used fictitiously. Also, all other names, places, locations, and incidents are entirely fictional, and any similarity to places or people living or dead is purely coincidental.

ACKNOWLEDGEMENTS

The first twelve chapters of this book were originally published as a monthly series in *Pest Management Professional* during 2018. I am especially grateful to Marty Whitford, Heather Gooch, and Leo Michael for bringing Crawley to life. Also, Oldham Chemicals Company, Memphis, Tennessee, sponsored publication of this book, and I am very grateful to Tommy Reeves for this support.

CHAPTER 1

Crawley and the Gnat Outbreak

It was a cool January noontime in a small town in central Tennessee. But the gnats were so bad, the preschoolers could barely eat their lunch. Hundreds of tiny bugs were dive-bombing their heads, darting toward their ears and eyes, and getting into their food. One of the children started crying, rubbing her eyes. "Ms. Johnson," she whined. "I think one of the gnats went in my eye."

"I ate one on accident," another said. "And now my stomach hurts."

"Okay children, even though it's cold, let's go outside to the playground. That should help. They seem to only be inside the building."

Ms. Johnson fought an urge to cuss. This had to stop. It was becoming a health hazard that might cause the facility to fail an upcoming health and safety inspection. Surely, somebody could get rid of these pesky gnats.

William "Crawley" McPherson, a pest management service technician for Peace-of-Mind Pest Services, got the call about the preschool building from his boss, Jackson "Jack" Blackwell. Crawley was never deterred by difficult insect problems. In fact, the weirder, the better. He had been a "bug man" for 12 years now and had seen more than his share of insect pests, vermin, and all manner of infestations. Sure, Jack had a fancy college degree in integrated pest management from Purdue University, but he didn't know about the intimate lives of insects like Crawley did — where they breed, their secret behaviors, and other mysterious facts that only Crawley would know by his years of detective-like inspections.

Today's situation was a strange one, all right. Jack had told him it was an old government building totally infested with tiny gnats, and he said even though it was winter, various kinds of gnats could potentially breed inside a dwelling. The building was occupied by three different agencies: a health department clinic, the local human services office, and a government-subsidized "Head Start" preschool program. Apparently, the gnat problem had been ongoing since last summer, and other pest management companies had tried unsuccessfully to solve the problem.

Upon arrival at the address, Crawley emerged confidently from the truck, donned his service belt containing an array of insecticidal baits and aerosol sprays, and swaggered toward the front door like John Wayne in a western movie, even though he looked nothing like the movie star. In fact, he could easily pass for Barney Fife. That's what he was all right, a Barney Fife pest man. A professional hitman for bugs. Not that he enjoyed killing things; he considered it an important profession. He liked to think that what he did made a difference. Helped people. Relieved suffering. Even prevented disease.

The receptionist was expecting his arrival: "Oh yes, we're glad you're here. I've been told to call Dr. Whittington immediately when you arrive."

At that, Crawley tried to display his most professional face and knew in his heart he was the man for the job. *Yeah, it's me. I'll get 'em.*

Dr. Caroline Whittington, who was a doctor at the clinic as well as director of the building, showed up holding a clipboard tight against her chest. Her face was hard, like that of a drill sergeant. This woman was not to be trifled with.

"I'm here to take care of your gnat problem, ma'am." He placed his right hand on one of the pesticides hanging on his belt. "Where they at?"

"I don't know what makes you think you can do any better than the other folks," she said dryly. "We've had five different exterminators out here to fog the place." Then she paused. "But I guess it won't hurt for you to try. We're at our wit's end."

Crawley pushed his thick glasses back up his nose and smiled. "But you ain't had me on the problem yet."

She looked him over, raising an eyebrow. "No, we haven't."

"This shouldn't take long," he said, hoping that would indeed be the case. Crawley had to act quickly. He didn't want Jack or Mary Jane "MJ" O'Donnell in on this case. Jack was the boss of the company, and MJ was one of the other top technicians working for Peace-of-Mind. He had to admit she was good. Her quick wit and stubborn Irish determination were hard to compete with.

"Just show me where they're at and I'll get rid of them," he said.

"They're everywhere," Dr. Whittington said sharply. "There's no one place where the gnats are located."

Crawley made a face. "Mmm. Well then, where are they worser?"

"Worser?"

"Yeah, like worse than worse. Like, one room where it's worser than the others."

The woman blew out a long breath, then turned and started down the hall. "Come this way."

Crawley followed her to the kitchen, but it wasn't just any kitchen. It was the mack daddy of all kitchens. Dr. Whittington turned and waved her arm. "This is probably where we see them more than anywhere, but like I said, they're all over the whole building."

Crawley's eyes suddenly looked like large ovals, roving around behind his thick glasses. Sure enough, he spotted what appeared to be small fruit flies darting around the inside of the room. "What do you use this kitchen for? This ain't no ordinary kitchen."

"I don't know what it was originally used for," she said, swatting at one of the gnats buzzing by her face, "but now we use it to prepare food for the preschool. As I told Mr. Blackwell when I called yesterday, three different groups use this building."

"How old are the kids, and how many of them you got here?"

"What difference does that make?" Dr. Whittington said dismissively, glancing at her watch. "Can't you just spray or fog the place and be on your way?"

"I've got to do a thorough inspection first, ma'am. That's procedure." Crawley looked at a row of doors along the west wall of the large room. "What's in all them rooms? Any mop closets? I've seen 'em come up outta drains before."

Dr. Whittington bit her lip as if trying to keep from saying something, then turned to go. "Well, feel free to do your little investigation, treat the place, and then leave. I've got patients to see."

"Inspection, ma'am," he hollered after the good doctor. "That's the first and most important step in the pest controlling process. After that, we'll decide what to do."

Crawley spent a good 45 minutes carefully inspecting the kitchen and all rooms connected to it for possible breeding sites of the gnats. In the process, he found a mop closet off to the side of the main room. He got down on his hands and knees and inspected the large drain in the floor with his flashlight.

"Mmm. I bet the trap in this thing is totally dried up."

He stood up and grabbed a few of the tiny flies darting about, and with a hand-held magnifying lens tried his best to identify them. They clearly weren't fruit flies. Perhaps they were scuttle flies, which some people called phorid flies. Whatever they were, there were hundreds of them everywhere.

He shook his head. This wasn't going to be an easy come-and-go fix like he had thought. If the drain trap was dried up, the mop closet was certainly a potential entry point. But from where? Was the place on a central sewer system? He placed a few of the gnats in a vial of alcohol for microscopic identification back at the office. He knew that a correct identification could lead to critical information about where they breed and other key facts about their life history. Proper treatment would depend on the species involved.

Crawley frowned. As much as he hated to, he would need to go back to the office, identify the flies, and then devise a treatment plan for the gnat problem. And that, of course, would mean having to involve Jack and MJ.

It was almost closing time when he pulled up to the Peace-of-Mind Pest Services office. A few service vehicles dotted the parking lot, although many of the pest technicians were allowed to keep company vehicles at their private homes overnight during weekdays, leaving the work parking lot mostly empty.

MJ O'Donnell met him just outside the front door. She was smartly dressed in her khaki Peace-of-Mind uniform. The only thing amiss was her red hair, being whipped around by the stiff, southern breeze.

"Did you do that stop at Linden and Eastover?" MJ asked. "That one with the preschool? I heard they've got a really bad gnat problem."

Crawley wondered how she knew all that. "Yep, already been there. I've got this one, MJ."

She tried unsuccessfully to swipe her hair back into position. "Did you find out what the problem is?"

"Working on it."

"You're being evasive. Did you find out where they're coming from?"

"You know my little saying on that, MJ. The one I learnt from a podcast by Jeff Tucker."

"I know, 'When you can't find the source of the bugs, keep looking. It's always there.'"

"Then that's my answer."

"You need my help?"

"Nope. Jack asked me to do the stop."

She smiled. "Indeed he did, but we make a pretty good team, don't you think?"

MJ was hard to resist for a lot of reasons, and he had to admit they had worked together on several difficult pest problems over the last few years. "Mmm. Let me look at them specimens I caught today and get back up with you."

She opened the door for him and smiled. "Sounds like a plan. I'd really love to help. I could bring you a Moon Pie as a bribe, you know."

As Crawley made his way down the hall to the bug examination room, Jack Blackwell emerged from his office, heading straight for Crawley. Jack was dressed in slacks, an almond-colored button-down shirt, and a wool sport coat. He could easily pass for a U.S. Senator.

Oh brother, thought Crawley. Here we go.

"Hey Crawley. I've been looking for you."

"Yes, sir. What for?"

"Did you service that government building on Linden?"

They must think that's the most important account in the world right now. "Yes, sir. Haven't made any treatments yet. I brought back some of the gnats for ID. Depending on that, I'll decide on a plan of action."

"Good. I can do the management plan, and even help with the identification if need be." Jack patted Crawley's shoulder. "I want to keep these people happy. It might lead to other government contracts. Be sure and keep me in the loop on this one. And I might need to meet you out there at least once, OK?"

Sure, you'll meet me out there. "Yes, sir."

The place was pretty much deserted by the time Crawley started the identification process in the bug room. He didn't care; he loved solitude. Just him and the bugs. He had spent many a night looking at bugs in the Peace-of-Mind examination room. They had it set up like a university laboratory, with white countertops lining the walls, hosting several nice, dissecting-type microscopes. In addition, there were two stacks of Cornell cabinets in the room, containing drawers of hundreds of properly identified insects. The reference collection was indispensable to Crawley, because he could always go find a "real" specimen of whatever he thought he had identified.

He placed a couple of the gnat specimens under a microscope and opened up the *Truman's Scientific Guide to Pest Management Operations*. He examined the gnats' eyes, antennae, legs, and the size and arrangement of spines on their body parts. These tiny flies were definitely not fruit flies, but he wasn't sure exactly what they were. He started "keying" them using the diagnostic key described in the textbook, which was essentially an algorithm designed to systematically eliminate choices until you're left with the correct one.

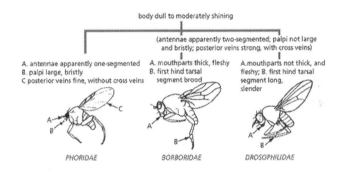

body dull to moderately shining

(antennae apparently two-segmented; palpi not large and bristly; posterior veins strong, with cross veins)

A. antennae apparently one-segmented
B. palpi large, bristly
C posterior veins fine, without cross veins

A. mouthparts thick, fleshy
B. first hind tarsal segment broad

A.mouthparts not thick, and fleshy; B. first hind tarsal segment long, slender

PHORIDAE   BORBORIDAE   DROSOPHILIDAE

Crawley turned to p. 333 of his *Truman's Guide, Seventh Edition,* and examined Fig. 14.1 to determine exactly what kind of Diptera specimen he had collected at the account.

Illustration: *Truman's Scientific Guide to Pest Management Operations* (Courtesy North Coast Media)

Crawley studied the creatures more closely. They all had large and conspicuous femurs or "thighs," meaning they were in the insect family Phoridae. He figured as much, based on the way he had seen them land and "skip" along the surface. He had learned that little tidbit about their behavior several years ago.

He sat back in the chair. Phorids. They're probably breeding in organic matter somewhere in or near the kitchen. Then he recalled something else he knew about them.

Phorids often are found in sewage leaking from broken pipes under buildings and situations like that.

I wonder if there's a broken sewer pipe near that kitchen?

Crawley was on-site at the government building by the time the first employees started arriving. He'd been sitting in his truck since 6:30 a.m., drinking coffee, eating honey buns, and listening to a pest management podcast about the life history of invasive filth flies.

He made his way to the kitchen to continue his inspection from yesterday. Crawley recalled how he had found the unused mop closet with a dried-up drain trap. Today, he intended to examine the area under the huge three-compartment sink, and especially the drain pipes coming from there. He slithered under the sink on the cold and clammy tile floor, looking for signs of leaks or build-up of scum and gunk in between the tiles. He focused his flashlight beam on the grout between tiles. *I've seen 'em breeding in cracks like this.*

Then he inspected the large pipe extending downward from the garbage disposal side of the sink. "Mmm. That could be a clue," he said softly.

Just then, he heard familiar voices approaching the kitchen. *Jack and MJ!*

He slid out from under the sink and stood to meet them. They were accompanied by Dr. Whittington. He tried his best to dust himself, straighten his uniform, and look presentable.

"This is where we determined yesterday that the gnats were most prevalent," Dr. Whittington said confidently to Jack and MJ. Crawley noticed how different the doctor was today with Jack around. She was much softer, even smiling. But one thing was the same: She looked right past Crawley, as if he didn't exist.

Her remark irritated him. We determined?

"I would probably agree with your determination," Jack said, smooth as any politician. "They're small flies, so they're most likely breeding inside the building. Doesn't matter that it's winter."

MJ smiled when she met Crawley's eyes, then nodded toward him.

At least she sees me here, working my butt off.

Jack began a circular tour of the room like a home inspector or real estate agent. "We've got to figure out where they're coming from. That's the first step in integrated pest management." Jack finally looked at Crawley when he got near him. "Did you determine the species?"

"Yes, sir. Members of the phorid fly family."

Jack nodded and turned back toward Dr. Whittington. "Just what I thought all along."

Crawley tried to hide his surprise.

Jack stopped at the big sink. "One thing we could try is some of that biological drain cleaner for these drains. There could be enough scum lining the pipes to breed phorids." He paused. "What do you think, MJ?"

"It's worth a try." She moved over by Crawley and smiled at him. "I'd like to hear what Crawley thinks about it. He's already done the inspection."

Both Jack and Crawley were surprised at her statement, but for different reasons.

"Yeah, uh, sure, that's right." Jack recovered from his gaff. "What have you determined, Crawley?"

This was his only chance. Crawley moved over by the sink and looked at Dr. Whittington. "Who uses this sink?"

"The preschool staff."

"Do they make stuff to eat for the kids every day?"

She didn't seem happy at the questioning. "Well yes, they do."

Crawley turned toward the wall where the sink was attached. "What's outside this here wall?"

"The outside, I presume. Grass?"

"Can we look and see?" He knew this might be a gamble.

"I guess." Dr. Whittington glanced at Jack. "But I don't see what difference it would make. Mr. Blackwell just said the gnats were most likely breeding inside."

Jack shrugged. "I guess it wouldn't hurt to take a look-see."

Outside the building, Crawley tried to line up with the kitchen by looking at the lone small window over the sink. Once he had done that, he stepped back in the yard about 20 steps from the building and started tapping the grass with his foot and scraping dirt side to side. He couldn't help noticing the others watching him curiously.

When he located a heavy, metal plate about the size of a large pizza in the grass, he turned to Dr. Whittington. "Can we get a maintenance person to lift up this plate?"

"Why? What does that have to do with anything?"

Crawley saw MJ smile and wink at him. *She knows.*

"Trust me, this here is very important."

After the doctor turned to go get someone, Jack lit in on him. "What are you doing, Crawley? Don't you realize that woman is the director of this place? You can't toy with her like that. We could lose the account."

"I know what I'm doing."

"You better!"

Momentarily, Dr. Whittington rounded the corner with a burly man following her. After a few tries, the man was able to pry open the lid with a crow bar, revealing a pit in the ground approximately the size of a garbage can. All kinds of pipes entered and exited the hole in the ground, leaving a vat in the middle holding a dark, slimy liquid. A column of millions of tiny gnats suddenly emerged from the soup-like goo, flying up toward the sky. Dr. Whittington and the others stepped back.

"It's a grease trap," Crawley said, smiling. "That's where they're at."

"But how are the gnats getting back into the building?" Dr. Whittington asked.

MJ beat Crawley to answer that one. "See all those open pipes?" She pointed. "Some of them probably go back into the kitchen. If there's a dried-out drain trap somewhere inside, it's like an interstate highway from here to there."

"Like a mop closet drain." Crawley displayed a big toothy grin, his eyes looming large inside his thick glasses.

"Yes, indeed, Dr. Whittington," Jack took it from there. "That's exactly the cause of your problem. We need to get this grease trap cleaned up and treated. Then we'll need to check all the drains in your building." His chest puffed out. "And then, after we do some space spraying with synergized pyrethrins, your problem will be solved."

"Wow!" Dr. Whittington said. "I had no idea …"

"That's why we're the best," Jack continued. "Come on, let's go back inside and I'll write up a detailed management plan."

On his way into the building, Jack turned back to Crawley and MJ. "I can handle this now. I need y'all to get on with your regularly scheduled routes." With that, he disappeared into the building with Dr. Whittington.

Crawley knew it would be this way. It always was. He turned to go to his truck, despondent. MJ reached out, placing her hands on his forearm. He could feel her warm hands through his long-sleeved shirt. "C'mon, Crawley. Don't take it that way. You solved the problem, and he knows it. Everybody does."

Crawley looked down. He desperately needed to hear her kind words. He tried his best to meet her eyes, but found it difficult. "Thanks, MJ. I appreciate it."

An impish grin spread across her face. "Let's go — you can help me with a fly problem at the Elmore Memorial Hospital."

"Inside or outside flies?"

"Uh, outside I think. At least that's what I've been told."

He knew she was just trying to get his mind off of Jack's snub. "Oh, there's not hardly any filth flies out in the middle of winter."

"You don't know that. Have you been out there and looked for yourself?"

"Well, naw."

"Then you're coming with me. We're not going to wallow in self-pity. Not today."

Crawley nudged his glasses back up his nose. Maybe she was right. There were lots of other pest cases out there to be solved.

CHAPTER 2

Crawley and the Dumpster Dilemma

"Look at this, Doctor," the nurse pointed at a wound near the patient's eye. With grave concern, she peeled back the bandage, revealing numerous cream-colored objects squirming around in a hole in the man's flesh. The hospital infection control doctor was horrified. He motioned for her to follow him out into the hall, where he lowered his voice. "I think they're worms of some kind."

"Worms?"

"Shh, keep it down. Can you imagine what'll happen if this gets out to the public?"

"Yes sir, that would be awful."

"Especially if the family finds out. They could file a lawsuit."

The doctor told her to go get a small penlight, forceps and an irrigation bottle filled with alcohol.

"Whatever they are, we've got to clean them out and get them identified."

While putting on latex gloves to do the procedure, the doctor seemed to be thinking out loud. "My gosh, where did these things come from, and how did they get in this patient? Don't we have pest control?"

Then he had another thought and turned to the nurse. "We need to get Environmental Services up here, stat! We need a thorough cleaning."

It was a cold February morning when Jack Blackwell, owner of Peace-of-Mind Pest Services, got the call about the problem in the nursing home wing of Elmore Memorial Hospital. Some kind of worms in a patient's wound. The man was an elderly invalid. That was bad enough by itself, but it was Jack's company that serviced the hospital. He had to do something right away, because the facility was a six-figure yearly account. He picked up the phone to call his technician, Brandon Mills, who serviced the hospital.

It didn't take Jack long to remind Brandon that pest control in healthcare facilities was extremely sensitive. Health department regulators could shut the place down for pest problems like this.

"Brandon, get out there to Elmore and find out what's going on. If bugs are showing up in patients' wounds, then we've got a serious problem somewhere."

There was a long pause on the other end of the line. "This is way beyond me, sir. Don't you think this is a job for Crawley?"

"He's good, but not very diplomatic. He might make waves among the management."

Brandon had an answer for that. "Yes, but you could send MJ with him. She's quite a people person."

"Great idea."

William "Crawley" McPherson drove as quickly as he could to the hospital. He popped a piece of watermelon-flavored hard candy in his mouth. He needed a shot of sugar for this case. He began to fantasize that his pest management truck was a brand-new police cruiser and he was some kind of SWAT team member headed to a fight. Adrenaline coursed through his system. This is what he lived for. He had never been deterred by difficult insect problems. Ever!

MJ O'Donnell was waiting for him at the front entrance to the hospital. All sorts of thoughts ran through his mind when his eyes hit her. But really, he experienced that every time he saw her. She was the most beautiful creature he had ever seen. Why she ever decided to become a pest control technician, he'd never know.

Crawley blushed when she opened the hospital door for him, and was careful to avoid eye contact. MJ was a diva who just so happened to know a great deal about bugs, both of which intimidated him.

He didn't want to feed the whirlwind of emotions swirling inside him, so Crawley shook his head to fling off the thoughts. He couldn't let himself think of her in that way. *She would never like a guy like me.*

"Hey, Crawley. Glad you're here." MJ waved her arm back toward the inside of the hospital. "This is gonna be a good one."

Crawley looked around. *Got to focus on the task at hand.* "Where they at?" he asked.

"This way," she pointed. "The east wing of the hospital where the elderly reside. That's where the patient with the bugs was located."

As they made their way through the hospital's maze of halls and elevators, Crawley's eyes darted around behind his thick glasses, trying to take it all in. There were hundreds of potential harborage sites and entry points for flies and other insects. His pulse quickened. It was overwhelming. Where should he start?

A smartly dressed man and woman met them at the main office on the first floor. Introducing themselves as assistants to the hospital administrator, they promised to aid in the investigation any way they could.

"And our hospital CEO has pledged his support in this matter," the woman added. "He said to tell you we'd provide anything you need. We've got to make sure this type of thing doesn't ever happen again."

"We appreciate that," MJ replied, smiling. "One thing we'll need right off is a map of all rooms on the wing and what they're used for. We've got to determine where flies or other insects are entering the building, and ways to intercept them before they reach the patients."

"We're just here to take care of your fly problem," Crawley said, oblivious to all the political pleasantries.

The man seemed taken aback at Crawley's abruptness. "Who said it's a fly problem?"

"It's obviously fly maggots related to a fly problem."

MJ's eyebrows went up.

"Well, I wasn't informed of that," the man said. "I only was told it was worms or bugs of some kind."

"Ain't no worms in a person's wound, but fly maggots sure can do that."

The man seemed to give up. "It's my understanding that the incident occurred in Room 235." He looked around. "We can escort you up —"

"Where's your dumpsters at?"

The man's eyebrows shot up and his cheeks reddened. All graciousness now evaporated. "I can assure you our trash disposal processes are well-run and attended to."

"Oh, I think Mr. McPherson is only suggesting that it's important for us to consider all aspects of the hospital environmental systems," MJ spoke calmly in Crawley's defense. "It's all part of our inspection process."

Crawley was undeterred, and made his way over to one of the big windows. "Mmm. Where's them dumpsters at? I've gotta look at 'em. And how could them flies be breeding outside during the winter?"

"But shouldn't we start with the patient's room?" the woman persisted. "That's where the problem is."

"Sure, I guess, but it don't make me no nevermind. I can guarantee that's not where the problem started."

MJ grabbed his elbow. "C'mon, Crawley, we probably should let these nice people show us the room where the event occurred," she soothed, "then we can look at the dumpsters. I promise."

As the foursome walked down the hall of the second floor, Crawley noticed that everything seemed unusually clean and orderly. There were certainly no flies buzzing about.

Crawley stopped by a large metal door on hinges in the hall that seemed to be a laundry chute. "Is this a laundry chute or a garbage chute?" He pushed on the bottom of the door, causing it to swing open toward the inside.

"Uh, you'll have to ask Environmental about that," the man said. "I think we may have both."

"Then where does the trash go?" Crawley asked pointedly.

The man shrugged, "Maybe it shunts it off toward the garbage dumpsters somewhere. Like I said, you'll have to ask them that."

Crawley blew out a long breath and started walking down the hall again. "Dumpster compactor chutes are a big problem, believe you me. There's all sorts of fly entry points goin' up and down 'em." Then he noticed an ultraviolet fly trap mounted on the wall outside the stairwell, so he stopped to check its glue board for captured flies. He knew that would be a good indicator of recent fly activity.

"Yeah, buddy!" Crawley grinned. "Lookey what I found." He displayed one of the dead flies between his thumb and index finger, which he had plucked from the glue board. He whipped out a hand lens with his other hand and examined the fly. "Uh hum, just who I thought you were ... Now to find out where you came from."

The man looked at Crawley like he was crazy.

"Oh, he just really gets into bug problems," MJ said. "Trust me, he'll figure it out and we'll take care of your problem."

Crawley continued examining the dead fly. "Uh oh, looks like *Chrysomya rufifacies*." He frowned. "The hairy maggot blow fly. They're bad ... and can cause myiasis."

MJ knew what he was talking about. That species was a common cause of fly maggot infestation in wounds, a condition called myiasis. But she also realized the administrative assistants were ready to show them the room where the patient had been located. "C'mon, Crawley. Let's go look in the room first."

Room 235 was empty and spotless, like a sterile lab room. There was no doubt the hospital administrator had ordered it cleaned and re-cleaned after the incident.

"Where's the patient?" MJ asked.

"We made arrangements to have him transferred to a private facility off-campus," one of the assistants offered. "That way, you guys can better inspect the room for fly breeding."

Crawley wondered about that. *Maybe just to get him outta here and keep the family from finding out what happened.* He walked to the window and tried again to orient himself to the layout of the building and grounds.

"Don't you think you should inspect the room for breeding sites instead of looking out the window?" the man asked.

Crawley whirled around and made a face. "Mmm. They must be from somewhere. They sure ain't coming from in here. It's too clean." He looked past the man, toward the door. "Where's the dumpsters, and how's the trash collected and taken out of here?"

The man took out his phone. "Let me call Environmental Services. They can deal with you on that. I think we've done about all we can do."

MJ intervened again. "Yes, maybe that would be the appropriate person or persons we need to work with in this important matter. We really appreciate your assistance."

After the administrative assistants left, MJ stood right in front of Crawley to get his full attention. "Please try to be more cooperative … and … courteous. You're going to end up causing us to lose this account."

"I don't care." He shook his head like a toddler. "They don't know nothin' about pest control. And I do." He brushed past her and headed to the window again. "I gotta find them dumpsters. That's where the problem is. I guarantee."

"Still," MJ insisted, "it wouldn't hurt to inspect the room and adjoining ones for flies, huh? We can do that while the Environmental people are on their way up here."

"I guess that'd be all right, but we ain't gonna find nothing. Them blow flies I found in that trap were coming this-a-way. Probably came up the stairwell."

"Yes, I'm sure you're right about that. But we can still look around."

Crawley shrugged and unwrapped another piece of candy. He needed more sugar.

Leon Williams soon showed up, finding MJ and Crawley in the bathroom inspecting tiles around the shower. "Hi there," he greeted them. "I'm the director of Environmental Services. Finding anything?"

MJ stood to shake his hand and waved out toward the patient room. "Let's go back out here. There's not enough room for three people in here."

Crawley followed them. *Talk, talk, talk. That's all everybody does around here.*

Mr. Williams began retelling the entire incident in an awkward way, obviously carefully choosing his words to put the hospital in the best light possible.

Crawley suddenly jumped up and walked out the door. *I'm going to find them dumpsters myself.* He darted to the stairwell and ducked inside, even though he heard MJ calling after him.

After 15 minutes of looking for Crawley up and down the halls of the unit, MJ decided it was time to call Jack. She hated to do it, but for all she knew, Crawley was in the administrator's office right now questioning him about trash disposal.

As usual, Jack seemed irritated that she called. "Talk to me, MJ," he said flatly.

"We need you down here at the hospital. Things aren't going as I thought they would."

"Okay, I'm listening."

"The Environmental people seem to be trying to control where we go and what we look at —"

"Probably for liability reasons."

"And I've lost Crawley," she blurted out.

"What do you mean, you've lost him?"

"He walked out when the people kept trying to tell us everything over and over. They obviously have a sanitized version of the incident."

"Oh Lord, I hope he's not stirring up trouble. I'm on my way."

"He's sweet, Jack. He wouldn't cause trouble."

"Maybe not on purpose, but trouble seems to follow him. I'll be there in a few minutes."

MJ and Mr. Williams met Jack outside the hospital.

"Hello, Jack." The man extended a hand. "I'm Leon, director of Environmental Services. You and I have met before."

"Yes, I remember you." Jack looked at MJ. "Is everything all right? Any luck finding the source of the infestation?"

"We've just been looking around the building and grounds while waiting for you."

"Crawley?"

"I presume he's investigating on his own somewhere."

A puzzled look crossed Mr. Williams' face. "Can't you just call him?"

MJ and Jack looked at each other. They both knew he wouldn't answer a phone call while on a case like this.

"Crawley earlier insisted we look at the dumpsters," MJ changed the subject. "Can we do that? Where are they located?"

When MJ realized Mr. Williams was confused, she tried to clarify. "We don't know the layout of this place. Our technician, Brandon Mills, usually services this account."

"Well sure, we can look at them," Mr. Williams said. "This way."

With that, he turned and headed straight inside the multi-story building.

MJ was shocked. *Dumpsters inside?*

Once in the building, the trio headed downstairs to a dungeon-like concrete area, with a sloping driveway from the main street to the basement.

Mr. Williams paused, and looked at MJ. "I can get you some disposable booties, if you like. It's pretty nasty down here."

She smiled, but shook her head, "No thanks. All part of the job."

"Suit yourself."

Further down the concrete slope, light coming from the outside partially illuminated a huge green compactor dumpster sitting in the middle of the room, with a garbage chute connecting it from above. The floor was coated with some type of gooey slime.

"Did this junk come out of that dumpster? Is it leaking?" MJ asked.

"They don't leak," Mr. Williams returned.

"How in the world do you empty the thing?"

"A truck comes down that slope, hooks up to it, and hauls it off twice a week."

Just then, they saw a flashlight beam bouncing erratically along the walls and beneath the dumpster. Then they spotted the outline of a crooked little man, bent over inspecting underneath the dumpster. *Crawley! How did he get down here?*

When they got to him, he was holding what looked like a popsicle stick coated with about a half-inch of black goo, as if he had been digging around under the dumpster. He displayed his usual big toothy grin. "I think this is where they're breeding at."

"How do you know that?" Jack asked. "Have you actually seen any maggots?"

"A few, but they're definitely up under there. I think this here dumpster box is old and cracked, and when they smash the garbage, stuff leaks out under it. Food, blood, and all sorts of stuff like that. That's perfect breeding grounds for fly maggots."

"I can assure you we have a contract with the dumpster company and they maintain it properly," Mr. Williams said, frowning. "I think they even clean out from under it once a week or so."

"No way," Crawley said. "There's all sorts of gunk and waste residue in the receptacle part of this thing, and also under it. Look, I'll show y'all."

He then lay down flat on the floor, sticking his head and right arm way up under the dumpster.

"Please don't do that," MJ hollered. "It's filthy down there."

All they could hear were garbled words coming from under the dumpster as he crawled further. Presently, he slithered back out and stood up, holding a big wad of dark goo about as big as a baseball.

"Look at your uniform!" Jack seemed indignant.

"I don't care." He was busy digging through the gooey mess looking for fly larvae, thrusting a goo-covered flashlight into MJ's hands. "Hold the light for me, please."

"Okay."

Sure enough, in the middle of the sample he had retrieved from under the dumpster, Crawley uncovered several creamy white, worm-like critters about a half-inch long. They were wiggling and writhing around in the gooey stuff. He carefully held up one of the maggots in MJ's light.

"Look at them little hairs on his body." He pointed with the other hand. "That means it's the hairy maggot blow fly."

Crawley puffed out his chest.

"I told y'all that's where they was at. They wasn't no need in spending all that time upstairs."

"But if you're right, how did the flies get upstairs into the patients' rooms?" Mr. Williams asked.

Crawley looked up and pointed. "When the adult flies emerge from these here larvae, all they gotta do is fly up that chute and go out through cracks, crevices and other openings into the hospital halls."

Mr. Williams seemed to be in shock. "Then what should we do?"

"You've got to clean all this up with a steam cleaner, spray the floor and walls with a good residual pesticide, and seal off all the —"

Jack interrupted. "I think we've seen enough." He reached for Mr. Williams' elbow. "You and I can continue this conversation in your office, Leon. I can write you up a detailed pest management plan."

Crawley fell silent.

When MJ saw the disappointment on his face, she pressed close to him and whispered, "It's okay, Crawley."

When they got back outside, Jack and Mr. Williams went one way and Crawley and MJ went another.

"You solved it, Crawley, and you know it." MJ tried to console him. "You said the problem was from the dumpsters all along. I'm proud of you."

"Mmm …" He didn't want to talk about it. Chalk another win up for Jack, and another setback for Crawley.

He sighed. Would he ever get the recognition he so desperately needed?

CHAPTER 3

Crawley and the Mysterious Itch

MJ O'Donnell was baffled by the case. This was one of her regular accounts — Alex and Shea Higginbotham — and they lived in a relatively new house with no history of significant pest problems. Now all of a sudden, both of them were complaining of biting pests … and their story seemed so believable.

It was mid-March as MJ made her way through the upscale Wellington District neighborhood, where the willow trees and redbuds were just beginning to put on leaves, one of the first signs of spring. She pulled up to their house on Primrose Street, and gathered her things to go inside for an inspection.

Alex Higginbotham greeted her at the door. He was friendly, but the look in his eyes belied his smile. "It's about time you got here, MJ. Come on in. Shea and I have been anxiously waiting for you." MJ couldn't help noticing numerous scabs and fresh bloody spots all over his hands and arms.

Oh, this is bad, she thought. "Are you still being bitten?"

"Worse than ever. Shea's been up all night cleaning and sanitizing everything. She thinks we're totally infested."

MJ was at a loss for a response. "I don't think they do that."

Alex held out his arms. "Then what's this?"

"I don't know." She paused. "But I'm here to try to find out."

"I appreciate it." He said flatly and opened the door wider. "Just go wherever you need to go and do whatever you need to do. But you need to put on some DEET repellent so you don't get 'em. We'll be in the living room eagerly waiting to hear your results."

The DEET repellent comment unnerved MJ, but she tried to reassure herself that she could walk through the house without getting infested. She found the house spotless. In fact, it looked like a museum, with everything perfectly in place and prominently displayed. It was as if they were trying to win the "best home interior award" in *Southern Living* or something.

The place smelled heavily of bleach. There was barely enough dust anywhere in the house for her to even collect one dust sample. She had serviced the account on several occasions previously, and had found no pets, no mice, no bird nests in the walls, or anything else that might lead to a mite infestation.

After a half-hour of attempting to take samples from around the house, MJ joined Alex and Shea in the living room. She was uncertain about sitting on the furniture, so she stood near the door.

"Please tell me again, Shea, when this started, and why you think it's an insect or mite problem."

"It started in the fall, before it got cold," Shea began, "when a bird accidentally got into the house." She looked over at her husband. "We think it came down through the chimney."

"A chimney swift, they call them," Alex offered. "Maybe it had built a nest or something in the chimney last summer. Anyway, it flew down one day instead of going up."

"We had a terrible time trying to catch that thing and get it out of here." Shea ran a hand through her hair. "It wasn't long after that when we started having problems. I think these bugs came off the bird and are now living in here. They're some sort of parasites."

"Are they just on you, Shea?" MJ asked. "Or both of you?"

"Well, on me first, I guess. Then Alex got them from me."

MJ looked from one to the other. It must be real since both of them have it, she thought. What are the chances two people could have something like this?

"Have you ever seen the bugs?" she asked aloud. "I mean, do you think you might catch one for me? I really need to see a specimen. Our treatment program depends upon a correct identification."

Shea shook her head. "We can't see them. I mean, sometimes we see little black specks on our skin, but I'm not sure what they are. Could be their eggs. Can't you just spray the house anyway?" She rubbed her arms obsessively. "We don't mind. We'll authorize it."

"I wish I could, but the state regulators won't allow us to make pesticide treatments without first identifying a target organism."

"Then what are you going to do?" Shea insisted. "We're being eaten alive." Her eyes filled with tears. "You've got to do something!"

MJ turned to leave. She didn't remember exactly what she said to Alex and Shea after that, but she definitely knew in her own mind what she was going to do.

This is a job for Crawley McPherson.

The next morning, MJ waited for Crawley near the front entrance of the Peace-of-Mind headquarters. She was sitting in a comfortable chair in the small foyer of the building, drinking coffee and pretending to read *Pest Management Professional* magazine, but she was really trying to ambush the little bug nerd when he arrived. She knew he usually came by the office early to get stocked up on pesticides for the day and get any last-minute instructions or assignments from Margie, the office manager.

Soon, she spotted him scurrying up the sidewalk toward the building. Sure, he was socially awkward and had disabilities, but MJ admired him. He was honest, hard-working and loyal. And he would go after a bug problem like a dog after a bone.

"Hey, Crawley!" She acted surprised to see him. "How's it going?"

His head finally came up, and he seemed to force a smile. "Okay, I guess ... don't know yet how it's going because it isn't going yet."

He walked nervously past her and started down the hall toward his office. MJ followed, trying to keep her tone light. "I've been missing seeing you lately. Where've you been hiding?"

He hesitated, turning halfway back toward her, as if he didn't know for sure what to do. "Just working, MJ. Trying to get it all done. Seems like Jack's always giving me someone else's account." Then a big toothy grin spread across his face. "But I really don't mind, it helps me be a better pest technician."

"You ever thought about taking the license exam and starting your own business?" MJ asked.

He blushed. "I guess … I might could try for a license." Long pause. "Maybe someday."

"Hey, speaking of you being such an expert, can I ask you about a case I'm working on?"

"Yeah, sure."

MJ looked up and down the hall. "C'mon, let's go in your office."

Inside Crawley's office, MJ told him about Alex and Shea Higginbotham and the mysterious pests biting them. She explained how none of her samples revealed any mites or biting insects that could produce bite marks on their bodies.

"I'm at a loss, Crawley," she concluded. "How do we help someone with a bug problem when we can't figure out what the bug problem is? I'm telling you, they're desperate."

"Sounds like you got a case of the DOP," he said flatly. "Those kind of folks'll drive you crazy."

MJ shook her head. "I don't think it's delusions of parasitosis. They both have bites all over their arms, hands, face and neck." She paused. "And according to them, also have bites all over their bodies under their clothing, but I didn't want to see any of that, if you know what I mean."

Crawley looked away. "Mmm."

"What do you mean by that?"

"It don't make me no nevermind." He looked away for a long time. "Did you set out glue boards?"

"Yes, repeatedly, but there's nothing on them but a few tiny beetles or an ant or two here and there. Mostly near the kitchen."

Crawley's eyebrows shot up. "Fire ants?"

"No, pharaoh ants, I think."

"Did you refer 'em to a dermatologist for them bite marks? That's the kind of doctor they need to see. Bites ain't nothing we do anything about."

"No, but that's a great idea. I'll call them and suggest that." She smiled at Crawley. "You want to go out there with me and look around? I'd really appreciate your help. Just having an extra pair of eyes to help look around would make me feel better."

"I guess I could work it in my schedule," he said, after some hesitation.

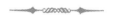

The next Saturday afternoon, Crawley made his way to the Higginbotham residence. Technically, he was off on Saturday afternoons, but it was the only time he had free to look at the Higginbotham case with MJ.

MJ was parked in the driveway when he arrived. He donned his technician's toolbelt, grabbed a small notepad, and went to meet her.

MJ flashed a huge grin. "I'm so glad you could come take a look, Crawley. You don't know how much this means to me. C'mon, they're waiting for us."

Alex Higginbotham met them at the door and ushered them into the living room, where Shea was sitting in a big fancy chair twice her size. She was angled to the side with her legs crossed. It reminded Crawley of Morticia of "The Addams Family," and he almost giggled out loud thinking about it.

Shea began by retelling the experience with the bird falling out of the chimney and how she was convinced that's how the bugs got inside the house. Then, she proceeded to describe in great detail how the mites would come and go, change in form and color, and submerge and then re-emerge in her skin on a nightly basis.

"I've got samples for you to look at on the dining room table," she said. "I did my best to collect some of the mites in pill bottles. I placed them in rubbing alcohol, I hope that's all right."

"That's great," MJ said. "We can look at them first before we perform the inspection."

Shea suddenly seemed even more grave and somber, as if some loved one had just died. "And you're not going to believe this," she continued, apparently not finished. "They go up inside our rectums when we're asleep."

"Shea!" Alex interrupted her. "They don't need to know that." He suddenly seemed deeply embarrassed. "Let's save that information for the medical doctors."

Shea fell silent, MJ's jaw dropped, and Crawley simply sighed. He'd heard talk like this before.

"Mites don't go up in peoples' rectum, ma'am. They don't do that. They'd die."

Shea's face reddened and the muscles in her jaw began to quiver. "Oh yes, they do!" Her voice became shrill. "You're not a medical doctor, how would you know?"

"I've read lots of medical books —"

Alex stood up and interrupted Crawley. "I've had enough of this. You're not going to talk to my wife like that. I think you should leave."

MJ tried her best to soothe things over. "Please excuse us." She shot an apologetic look toward the couple. "Crawley's just trying to help. He's our best technical expert."

Alex headed toward the front door, as if he intended for Crawley and MJ to follow. "Well, if he's all you got, we need to look somewhere else for help with our pest problem. And you call yourself Peace-of-Mind?"

"Look," MJ pleaded, "I'm sorry, I know you're upset. I invited Mr. McPherson to help me figure out what kind of bug problem you have. Couldn't you at least allow him to look around? He really is an outstanding entomologist."

Alex turned, arms tight across his chest. "Since you invited him, I'll allow it this time, but to be totally honest, I don't want him to ever come back."

The scene sent Crawley back to his childhood days when his dad would scream at him for forgetting to do his chores or not cleaning his room. It was all he could do to stand there in the Higginbotham home and not run out the door. Shea huffed and shot out of the room, saying something about going out on the patio to clear her head.

"Thank you. Thank you so much," MJ gushed. "We'll make a quick inspection and then be on our way."

MJ caught up with Crawley in the dining room where the Higginbothams had displayed their samples. She looked at him sympathetically. "You okay?"

"They didn't have to act so ugly," he mumbled, while looking through the pill bottles and resealable sandwich bags on the table. He held a few of the samples up to the light and examined them one by one with a small hand lens. "I could just leave here and never come back. It's not my account, you know."

"Yes, I agree it was uncalled for, but don't you think you were a little blunt with them? These are our customers. We've got to treat them right."

"I know I shouldn't a' said it. Something just flew all over me when she was saying all that. But I was just tellin' the truth, MJ. There ain't no bugs can come and go in a person's rectum. And these here samples are just lint, debris, and skin scabs. This is clearly a case of DOP, and you know it."

"I'm starting to see that now," she said quietly, looking around to make sure no one was listening, "but what are we going to do?"

"You gotta walk away from it, MJ. Otherwise, it's a time sink you'll never get out of. I've seen this over and over. They'll just keep bringing in more samples and insist you spray the house."

"But they're my account. Do I just quit servicing their house? They'll go to another pest control company."

"Let 'em," he said. "We're bug people, not doctors. These folks need to go see a dermatologist doctor. This ain't no bug problem. Simple as that."

After a long minute, MJ answered. "I guess you're right. "Let's go. I'll tell them we're going to take these samples back to the lab for closer examination and get back with them about the results."

On the way out to their trucks, MJ stopped to face Crawley. "I really appreciate your help with this. I knew something about this case didn't make sense, but I thought since both of them had symptoms, it had to be real. That's why I asked you to help."

"That's called a *folie à deux*, MJ. Two crazy people, or two persons with some kind of shared delusion. One gets it first, and then somehow convinces the other one that they are also infested. Happens all the time."

"Where in the world do you get this stuff?" MJ raised her hands. "How do you know such things?

Crawley's eyes danced around behind his thick glasses. "Mmm."

MJ seemed relieved. "Like I said, meet you back at the office. We can look at their samples to make sure there's nothing there, then I'll call them and that'll be the end of it. I'll tell them this could a medical issue and they may need to see a dermatologist. If they want us to continue their general pest control services, fine. Otherwise, they can find another pest control company."

She paused, then reached for his hand. "C'mon, I'll buy you a drink at my Uncle Kelly's pub."

"I'm not much of a drinker."

"Doesn't matter. You can get a soft drink, or even milk, if you like. We can visit a while. It'll be fun."

CHAPTER 4

Crawley and the Humongous Cockroaches

Oh no, there's bugs all over her! Help! Help! Nurse, come help! They're everywhere — even on her face," screamed a patient.

Jacqueline, a nurse's aide, ran into the room. "I'm here, Miss Gertrude. Calm down." She looked around the room. "It's OK. Maybe you just thought they were bugs."

She wheeled the patient back to the other side of the room. "Now let me check Miss Vivian to make sure everything's all right. I'm sure whatever it was is gone now."

"But I saw 'em! They were humongous. I saw 'em."

Ten minutes later, Jacqueline was in the nursing coordinator's office. "I know these Alzheimer's patients can be confused sometimes, but I've seen some really big cockroaches in that room myself lately. What are we going to do?"

Her boss barely looked up. "Report it to facilities management, but other than that, keep this incident to yourself, if you know what I mean."

"Yes ma'am."

Later that day, Jack Blackwell, owner of Peace-of-Mind Pest Services, got a call from the nursing home. Upon hearing about the cockroach problem, Jack expressed grave concern and promised to get someone out there right away. As soon as he hung up, he tapped in MJ O'Donnell's mobile number.

"MJ, don't you have Pleasant Hill Nursing Home out on Monroe Street?"

"Yes, Tony Ellherd and I shared it, before he retired at the end of the year. Now it's all mine. Why?"

"I just got a call that they're having problems with cockroaches. They said they were huge mamma-jammas. Can you go by there and see what's going on?"

"Sure, I know that facility well. I don't think they have a cockroach problem, unless something's changed. I work hard to keep the place treated appropriately."

"Well, apparently they've got a problem now. Go check it out … and take Crawley if you need him. He loves things like that." Long pause. "Even with his faults, he's turned out to be a real asset to our company."

"You did the right thing hiring him, Jack. He's smart and I really like him."

"I'm sure you do," Jack said flatly. "But you have to admit, sometimes his mouth overloads his rear end. Now go out there and see what you can do, and report back to me."

Pleasant Hill Nursing Home was neither pleasant nor on a hill. It was an older facility located at the edge of an abandoned, city-owned lot next to the industrial park. MJ made her way across double railroad tracks and turned into the large, spacious parking lot of the medical facility. Tufts of grass were growing through cracks in the concrete all across the lot. She looked around before getting out of her truck, even though she had been there many times. *I don't think I'd want any of my relatives in this place,* she thought.

Inside, she made her way to the administrator's office. Felix Applewhite rose from his desk to meet her. He looked like a man from the wrong decade, wearing a dark green three-piece polyester suit, complete with a button-up vest. "Hello there, Ms. O'Donnell. What brings you out here today?"

"Hi Felix. My boss said someone reported a cockroach problem, so I came to do an inspection."

He looked at her blankly. "That's news to me. I don't know who would call that in. We don't have any roaches. Believe me, I would know. We run a tight ship around here. 'No hazards or harm to our residents' is our motto."

MJ nodded, even though she knew Mr. Applewhite wouldn't know if they had cockroaches, snakes, or even alligators in the nursing home because he never visited the patient rooms. He was an accountant by training and always had his head in the books.

"Well, I'm going to look around a bit and then let you know what I find out."

He sat back down and looked at his paperwork. "You can just report your findings to facilities management unless it's something really drastic. I really don't have to know everything. I don't micromanage this place, you know."

On her way down the hall, MJ considered what she had just heard. She shook her head in disbelief. The man was full of contradictions, saying all that about running a tight ship and knowing if they had roach problems, and then later saying he didn't micromanage the place.

The first place she stopped was the nurses' station and break room. MJ had learned through the years that pest problems in healthcare facilities often originated in staff lockers and break rooms. Many times she had found rotting or spoiled fruit, half-empty soda cans, and partially eaten snack cakes in these areas.

MJ inspected the lockers with a flashlight, then the break table, along the baseboards of the room, and lastly around the garbage can. Then she lifted the garbage bag out of the can for a peek under it. She knew there could be gunk in the bottom of the can from leaking garbage bags. Surprisingly, everything was quite clean and tidy.

Just then, a young woman walked in. MJ could see by the nametag that she was a nurse's aide named Jacqueline.

"Hi Jacqueline, I'm from the pest control company doing an inspection."

"Oh hi," Jacqueline grinned real big. "Glad to see you. We've been seeing a lot of roaches lately."

"Oh yeah? Where?"

She hesitated, biting her lip. "Mostly in the Alzheimer's Unit, but only inside the patient rooms and out in the hall. Never up in the beds or anything."

MJ studied her. What a weird thing to say.

"Can you show me exactly where?"

Jacqueline looked out toward the hall nervously. "I guess that might be all right."

MJ followed Jacqueline down the hall until it turned right and angled back toward the west. Jacqueline opened two sets of sturdy double doors by swiping her ID card through an electronic badge reader. MJ recalled being in this Alzheimer's Unit on previous pest control service stops, but this time it seemed different.

"Have y'all changed this wing? I don't remember it looking like this last time I was here."

"Yes, they just recently finished updating the doors, installing cameras, and adding new security systems. Now it's like going in and out of a prison."

"What about the food? Isn't that a pain to bring food carts down here from the cafeteria three times a day?"

"I'm not sure how they do that." She turned her head to the side. "To be honest, I don't want to know."

Jacqueline turned into one of the patient rooms occupied by two elderly women, one seemingly unconscious in the bed and the other sitting in a wheelchair.

After Jacqueline introduced MJ to Miss Gertrude, the patient in the wheelchair, and explained the purpose of her visit, she waved her arm back toward the room. "This is one of the rooms where I've seen cockroaches. Feel free to look around and do whatever you need to do." She turned toward the door. "I've got to get back to work."

"Wait," MJ said, taking a step toward Jacqueline. "Just one more thing: What are in the rooms immediately next door on either side of this one? I noticed one of them doesn't look like a patient room."

"Not sure … maybe storage." Jacqueline seemed even more uncomfortable. "I've got to go. Really."

After Jacqueline left, MJ inspected the room and attached bathroom. She was careful to not upset Miss Gertrude, who studied her every movement. MJ found a few dried roach feces in one corner of the room.

"Have you seen anything unusual in your room lately?" MJ asked.

"Well no, I don't guess." Miss Gertrude suddenly looked out the window. "Young lady, they're not nice to people around here, you know. Can you help me out to my car? I'm supposed to meet my son Harold this afternoon."

MJ knew better than to fall for that. "No ma'am, I'm just the pest control person. You'll have to ask one of the nurses about that."

"Pest control?" Miss Gertrude's eyebrows shot up. "I've been seeing lots of humongous roaches in here lately, and mice and rats."

"Really?" MJ was taken aback. "Roaches and rats and mice?"

"Oh yeah, hundreds. And one of the rats told me a secret about this place the other day."

"Well, don't you worry one little bit," MJ said cheerfully. "We'll work hard to get rid of them for you."

MJ excused herself, went back out into the hall, and went to inspect the rooms on either side. One was another patient room, but the one on the east side had a different type of door. It was locked, and no one she was able to find in the hall knew where a key might be.

After checking the nurses' station in that wing and the dumpsters outside without seeing any cockroaches, MJ decided she had done all she could. Things didn't add up. Perhaps she should consult Crawley. He would know what to do.

Three days later, Crawley was scheduled to meet MJ in the parking lot of the nursing home. He had agreed to help her investigate the cockroach infestation. Of course, he didn't mind helping her, but the box of banana-flavored Moon Pies she promised him sealed the deal.

He smiled thinking about it. Sugar always works.

Crawley put on his service belt and walked toward MJ's truck. He noticed how the April sun seemed higher in the sky than it had lately. Spring was definitely here; summer would soon follow. He found MJ sitting inside the cab entering something in her handheld computer. She rolled the window down.

"Oh hi, Crawley. Thanks so much for coming." She looked back at the computer. "Give me a second to close this file."

Crawley looked at her truck. It was a great example of what a pest control vehicle should look like — clean, orderly and professional. He smiled when he saw a big plastic daisy in a short vase on her dashboard. She always put a personal touch on things.

Presently, she packed up and exited the truck. "You ready?"

"Yep, but I'm not sure why you need me."

MJ took off toward the building, leaving Crawley struggling to keep up.

"You'll see," she said. "There are conflicting statements from the patients and staff. Some say they've seen lots of cockroaches, while others say there's no problem whatsoever. Apparently, the roach problem — if there is one — is concentrated in the Alzheimer's Unit."

"Any storm sewers around the place?"

"Not that I know of."

"Where are the dumpsters in relation to the Alzheimer's Unit?" he asked next.

"Too close, I have to admit. Near the back entrance, but it's an emergency exit. Nobody goes in or out that way."

"That wouldn't matter to a cockroach. They can enter through a crack."

MJ stopped to push the buzzer at the front door to gain access. "That's exactly why I need your help. You think like a bug."

After some pleasantries with the woman at the receptionist desk, MJ asked for someone to escort them to the Alzheimer's Unit.

A young man in blue scrubs showed up and politely guided them through several sets of secure doors into the Alzheimer's Unit.

"Is there anything else I can do for you?" he asked when he got them to their destination.

"No, thanks so much," MJ said. "You've been very helpful."

With that, the man turned and disappeared down the hall.

"Does everybody have to go through all them security doors to get in here?" Crawley asked. "Even the workers?"

"Apparently so," MJ said.

"Seems kinda cum'ersome."

MJ looked up and down the hall. "Now, we need Room 122, the room I was in the other day," she stopped and pointed. "Oh, there it is. Let's start there."

Inside the room, they found the invalid patient who seemed totally oblivious to their presence, and Miss Gertrude, staring out the window from her wheelchair.

"Good afternoon, Miss Gertrude," MJ said loudly, but gently.

The woman whipped her head around. "Are you here to give me my medicine?"

"No ma'am. We're from pest control. You may not remember me from the other day."

"Well no, can't say as I do. I can't remember all you nurses."

MJ glanced over at Crawley. There was no need in trying to explain it.

"Do you mind if we look around a few minutes?" she asked.

"Go ahead." After a few seconds the woman added, "If you're a new nurse, I'll say one thing — they don't treat people right in here."

Crawley went off to inspect the bathroom, leaving MJ to handle Miss Gertrude. He'd seen people with dementia many times while servicing healthcare facilities. He never knew what to say. Socializing wasn't his thing.

In the bathroom, he carefully examined the floors, tiles in the bathroom walls and floor, and then lastly, a cabinet under the lavatory sink. He found all sorts of supplies in the cabinet, including toilet paper, liquid soap, and even liquid cleaners.

Crawley shook his head. "They ought not have these things here. Them Alzheimer's patients might eat or drink them."

He was finally able to move the stuff aside well enough to see the back wall of the sink cabinet.

"Uh oh." Where the sink drainpipe entered the wall, there was almost 2 inches of open space around the pipe. He knew that was an interstate highway for insects and rodents.

He shined his light into the opening and thought he spotted a large, reddish-brown cockroach scurry away.

"American cockroach," he muttered.

Back in the main patient room, he found MJ kneeling down and inspecting the baseboards. She stood up when he came in. "Find anything?"

He tipped his head toward the hall. "I'm done. You ready to go?"

MJ must have gotten the message because she quickly said goodbye to Miss Gertrude and headed out into the hall.

Once outside the room, Crawley told her about the large opening under the sink where the drainpipe exited the bathroom and how he thought he had seen an American cockroach.

"That cabinet had a lock on it the other day, and no one could find a key," MJ sighed.

"Well, there was no lock on it today, so the nurses must've forgotten to put it back on."

"Ugh," she shook her head. "We can at least insist they get that hole fixed."

"The more important thing is, where does that opening lead to?" Crawley asked. "That's where the mother lode is."

"I don't know — oh, but that reminds me. Look here at the room on the left." MJ pointed toward the one on the left side. "That one is locked, and no one could let me in last time. My floor plan of the building says it's a just another

patient room, which I think it still was the time before I was
here — but Tony usually did this side of the facility. I know
they've replaced the doors and such recently, and I have a
feeling this room's use has been changed, too. I wonder what
it's for now?"

"Mmm."

"What?"

"That's the side where the drain pipe enters the wall."

Crawley jiggled the door handle. Then he got down on
his knees and tried to look under it. Then he popped back
up. "I think I smell food in there."

"Food? No way."

MJ got down on her knees beside him and sniffed the
bottom of the door. "Hmm, maybe."

"We've got to get inside there, MJ."

MJ took off down the hall toward the nurse's station, where she again requested someone give them access to the room.

Presently, the same man in scrubs showed up, and MJ explained to him that she and Crawley needed to get inside the room for a pest inspection.

"It's my understanding that room is inaccessible," he said.

"What do you mean, 'inaccessible'?" MJ asked impatiently. "We have the pest control contract on this place. We can look in any room we want."

"I think it's dry storage, and uh, they have some things in there that need to be inaccessible to patients in this unit, if you know what I mean," he said hastily.

"But we ain't patients," Crawley edged in between MJ and the man.

"I understand that," he said, "but if we open that door, the patients will see that the room is there and then be obsessed with getting inside. You just don't know how these people are."

"That makes no sense whatsoever," MJ snapped as she pulled out her phone. "I'm calling facilities management, they'll let us in."

The man turned to go. "Good luck with that."

Presently, an older, stocky man showed up with a wad of keys on his side as big as a softball. He smiled when he saw MJ. She remembered he was the facilities management supervisor, named Doug.

"I remember you," he said. "You're the woman from Peace-of-Mind Pest Control. We met one time when we were having a mouse problem in the kitchen."

MJ smiled weakly. "Yes, I remember, Doug. Look, we need to get inside this room to perform an inspection. There's been a cockroach problem in this wing and we're trying to figure out where they're coming from."

"There's no need to go in there. It's just dry storage."

"I don't care if it's dry storage, wet storage, or totally empty. If you want us to continue to be your pest control company, you're gonna have to let us look in there."

Doug hesitated, as if weighing the pros and cons of continuing the argument, then relented. "Suit yourself. I just work here. I'm not the one who decided how to use this room." He unlocked the door and stepped aside.

Inside, Crawley and MJ were shocked. Sure enough, the room did contain dry storage — stacks of boxes along two of the walls, but in the middle of the room were three food carts from the cafeteria, containing trays of half-eaten and spoiled food. Several big American cockroaches scurried away from the trays toward a 3-inch hole in the west wall's drywall near the ground, the result likely of a heavy box falling off a cart and banging into it.

Crawley shot over to the hole in the wall to get a closer look. "This is where they're coming from."

"Gross!" MJ exclaimed and turned toward the man from facilities management. "What's this all about?"

Doug shrugged. "It's not my fault. We told 'em they shouldn't do it."

"Who? Who put these carts in here?"

"The aides from the cafeteria."

"Why?"

"I don't know, I had nothing to do with it."

"We need an explanation, Doug." She reached for her phone again. "Or I'll need to call the health inspector."

Doug raised his hands. "The cafeteria folks said it was too difficult for them to take the food carts back and forth all the way down to this wing through all those special security doors three times a day. That's six trips through the security doors each day, so they asked could they leave them in here and just take them all out once a day."

Crawley spun around. "But these here carts have been left in here more than one day."

Doug shrugged again. "I can't explain that. That's the cafeteria folks."

Crawley started for the door. "I'm going out to the truck to get my sprayer and several tubes of cockroach bait. I'm gonna spray a good residual up in that hole in the wall, and then put out bait in cracks and crevices in this room and the adjoining ones. After that, y'all are gonna have to fix that hole."

Doug's eyes grew big at the mention of pest control products. "What about the patients?"

"I've got bait products specially made for sensitive accounts like this," Crawley said. "It won't hurt nothin'."

MJ was full-on angry at the situation, remembering Miss Gertrude's fears. "And soon, we're going to have to have a 'come to Jesus' meeting with your cafeteria folks," she told Doug. "This has got to stop."

Doug crossed his arms. "Don't kill the messenger. I didn't do this."

"Yes, but you knew about it," MJ said. "That's just as bad. This room is a breeding site for cockroaches and no telling what all else. They could be transmitting germs to the patients."

Doug rounded up cafeteria staff members to come remove the food-laden trays and wipe down the walls and floors, after which Crawley was able to apply pesticide treatments in the room. Meanwhile, MJ tried calling Felix Applewhite, the nursing home administrator. Of course, he was "suddenly called downtown" for a meeting. She rammed her phone in her back pocket. She would have a discussion with him later.

After they were satisfied that the treatment was workable and the staff would no longer be using the stockroom as a holding tank for meal leftovers, MJ and Crawley walked out to their trucks.

"Thank you, Crawley, for being here with me today," MJ said, clasping his forearm. "It means a lot to me."

"Oh, I didn't do nothin'."

"You did. You solved the problem."

He smiled widely. "It's all in a day's work, MJ. All in a day's work."

CHAPTER 5

Mystery Bugs in the Poultry House

It didn't seem to matter that it was May, and hadn't been warm long enough to create large insect populations yet. Bugs were everywhere in the commercial farm's poultry house. Not thousands, not hundreds of thousands, but *millions* of them crawled around on the walls. They dropped from the ceiling, into the nesting boxes and on the wooden slats that made up part of the floor of the breeder-broiler house. A worker in charge of taking eggs off the conveyor belt was in tears when the corporate veterinarian, Dr. Christi Anniston, interviewed her about her working conditions.

"They're everywhere!" she blurted out. "And they get on everything, even my clothes. What kind of bugs are they?"

"I'm not sure," Dr. Anniston said gently. "I'm not an entomologist, but my best guess is baby cockroaches. I'm going to take samples today and try to get them identified."

The veterinarian walked outside, where the sunlight temporarily blinded her. She had seen pest problems in poultry houses before, but never like this. Something needed to be done. This was becoming a health hazard that might harm the chickens as well as the farm workers. Surely *somebody* could get rid of these pesky insects.

⸻⸺◈◈◈⸺⸻

Later that day, Jack Blackwell, owner of Peace-of-Mind Pest Services, got the call about the pest problem at the poultry farm. Even though he didn't do agricultural pest control, he certainly would be glad to help any way he could. Besides, Jack was always looking for new ways to expand his pest control business — and word might get around to the farm owner's friends that Peace-of-Mind could help with their pest problems.

On the phone, as Dr. Anniston described "millions of tiny bugs" in the poultry house, Jack racked his brain trying to think what they could be. Maybe they were litter beetles, a common problem affecting poultry production, but from what the veterinarian described, these bugs were more soft-shelled than beetles. Either way, by the time he hung up, Jack knew exactly which of his technicians would be perfect for this job: Crawley McPherson. Crawley was a bug fiend who could find and solve any pest problem, anywhere.

"Crawley, we need you to go out there to the Johnson Farm on Old 82 Drive and find out what's going on," Jack told Crawley by phone, as the latter was wrapping up a visit on his regular route. "They've got a real bad bug problem. Dr. Anniston, the corporate veterinarian, is your point of contact and she's collected some of the bugs for identification."

There was a long pause on the other end of the line. "We don't do poultry house pest control, Jack. Never have before.

I think that's up to the particular chicken company or maybe even the Department of Agriculture."

"I know, Crawley, but this might be different. I think this farmer provides living quarters for his migrant workers. That would be a new account for us, and could lead to others out there in the area."

Jack waited a few beats before adding, "Besides, isn't it true that you're certified in almost every single commercial category except fumigation?"

"Well yeah, but I just did that for the fun of it."

"Then go out there and talk to that veterinarian and the chicken farmer. We're not going to charge them anything — we're just looking around, so to speak, friend-to-friend."

"Mmm."

"You don't agree?" Jack fought back his irritation. Sure, Crawley was by far the smartest technician he had ever had, but subordination … well … that was a different story.

"Didn't say that. I like a challenge, but I ain't understanding why we're servicing commercial poultry production."

"Didn't you hear me? I didn't say we were servicing poultry production. Look Crawley, just go out there today and see if you can help them figure out what the problem is. That's all."

"Yes, sir."

Crawley drove as quickly as he could to the chicken farm to investigate the bug problem. He fished a banana-flavored Moon Pie out of his glove box and wolfed it down. Didn't matter how old the thing was — he needed some quick sugar for this case.

Crawley had studied for state certification in Category 1, Agricultural Pest Control, and knew about litter beetles occurring by the millions in poultry houses. But he had never actually visited a chicken farm to see for himself. Jack's description of bugs at the chicken farm seemed weird, but to Crawley, weird was cool.

The farmer, Ben Johnson, was standing just outside the poultry house when Crawley pulled in the driveway. He was a burly man with a deep tan and with muscles in places Crawley didn't have. Crawley emerged from his truck and donned his service belt, which contained a flashlight, screwdriver, moisture meter, and several small cans of aerosol pesticide.

"Uh, I'm Crawley," he introduced himself. "I'm here to help with the bug problem — uh, I mean to look at it for you."

"I certainly hope so," Mr. Johnson said. "There's a bazillion of them in there."

"Then they won't be hard to find," Crawley said with a smile. "What kind a' harm they doing?"

"They're bothering the chickens, 'cause I've seen them on 'em. And my egg production is down."

He looked at Crawley in a condescending manner. "But that's not something you would know about, I suppose."

Crawley was used to people thinking he was stupid because of his looks and lack of social skills, so it wasn't hard to ignore the insult. "Where're they at? Let's take a look at 'em."

The man pointed at the entrance to the football-field-long white poultry house. "You can go in right there and see them all you want. But first, you've got to put on coveralls, booties, hair nets, and gloves. Can't have you infecting my chickens with anything, you know."

Entering the building was like walking into a huge department store, except with nothing on the floor but two rows of metal chicken nesting boxes in the middle. A conveyor belt connected them all, heading back toward a front office. The rest of the entire building contained thousands of chickens crowded into the open floor area. They scattered in front of Crawley and the farmer like a living wave as the pair walked through the birds. Within 10 ft. inside the huge chicken house, Crawley spotted bugs about the size of apple seeds all over the walls and ceilings.

He made his way through a big wad of birds to get a closer look at the wall where the bugs were.

"Uh oh!" Crawley now knew what they were. *Bed bugs!*

He pinched one between his index finger and thumb, then made his way back to Mr. Johnson in the middle of the room. "Look here at this." He released the bug from between his fingers and showed the man. "I think it's a bed bug, but I've got to check them back at the lab to make sure."

Mr. Johnson was astonished. "Bed bugs? I've never heard of them getting inside poultry houses."

"Yep, I've read about it." Crawley nodded. "Especially in organic poultry operations and breeder-broiler houses like this here one."

"So they're sucking blood outta' my chickens."

"Yes sir, probably so, every night. Suckin' 'em dry."

Mr. Johnson fell silent, and there they were, two grown men staring at each other, dead-still in the middle of thousands of gyrating, clucking chickens. It was as if Crawley had just told the man that the moon was made of cheese.

"No wonder my egg production is down." He shook his head. "What can we do about it?"

Crawley looked up at Mr. Johnson, his eyes like large ovals roaming around behind his thick glasses. "That's the problem, sir, there ain't much can be done, as long as these here chickens are around. You can get someone to spray the bugs when the birds are sold off and the house is empty."

"That might be Thanksgiving!" The big man shook with frustration. "What am I supposed to do until then?"

Crawley didn't have an answer to that, so he headed back toward the wall to collect specimens to confirm the identification back at the office. He knew there was a slim chance they could be bat bugs instead of bed bugs. Then, he would discuss the problem with MJ and Jack.

Back at the office in the examination room, Crawley looked through a microscope at the bed bug specimens he had collected. He carefully checked the pronotum area immediately behind their tiny heads to see how long the setae were. He knew the main identifying characteristic of bed bugs was the length of the pronotal setae. The setae were twice as long in bat bugs as they were in true bed bugs. In this case, there was no mistake: The setae were short, characteristic of true bed bugs.

wing pads narrow
at inner margin

COMMON BED BUG

wing pads broad
at inner margin

BAT BUGS

Crawley could confirm his findings by turning to p. 320 of his *Truman's Guide to Pest Management Operations, Seventh Edition* (Figure courtesy North Coast Media).

Crawley pushed his chair back and sighed. "Bed bugs. It would have been better if they were bat bugs." He paused a long time. "Much easier to explain … and for sure, easier to treat."

Just then, Jack walked in, followed soon by MJ. Jack drilled him with his eyes. "Crawley, what do you think about the bugs in Mr. Johnson's poultry house?"

"They's bed bugs."

Shocked, Jack shook his head. "That's really bad, but I should have known. I've seen presentations on this kind of thing at the national pest control meetings."

MJ chimed in. "What're our options for treatment?"

"Heat is often used for hotels and apartments," Jack said. "I guess we could try to find someone with a special license for agriculture who could do a heat treatment for them."

"No matter who you find licensed in whatever category, it ain't gonna work." Crawley looked down. "Poultry houses are way too big to heat up to the proper temperature and hold it for hours. Besides, the chickens are still in there for a few more months."

"We can get someone to spray the houses — all cracks and crevices — with pesticides," Jack was undeterred. "That might do the trick."

Crawley stood up and started walking around the room. "Might help, but won't eliminate them. They're everywhere in there. I saw lots of them way up high on the ceiling. I think you would need some kind of liquid spray to douse the inside of the house that wouldn't hurt gettin' on the chickens. That might buy the farmer some time."

MJ rubbed her chin. "We can't make chemical applications in there, and especially not to animals, Crawley. You know that."

"No, we can't," Crawley smiled, "but *somebody* can. I think the chicken companies have licensed people that spray the houses, and there are certain products labeled for sprayin', even with birds in there."

Jack shook his head in amazement. "How would you know things like that, Crawley?"

No response. He sat back down at the microscope and began looking at the bed bugs again.

"How *would* you know such things?" MJ asked in a tone much gentler than Jack's. "It's not in any of our training manuals, not even the *Truman's Guide*."

He raised up, eyes hovering slightly above the microscope eyepieces. "Stuff like that's on the Extension Service website under 'poultry pests.' Haven't y'all read it?"

MJ and Jack glanced at each other, then Jack issued instructions. "OK, then, Crawley, I want you to type up for me a list of options, pesticides and subcontractors we might could give Dr. Anniston. And find out who can spray inside the house with live birds present. Get it to me by tomorrow, close of business."

"Mmm." Crawley returned to looking through the microscope. "There ain't nothing will work until the birds go out in the fall. You'll see."

Three days later, Crawley and MJ met Mr. Johnson, Dr. Anniston, and other representatives from the Service King Poultry Co. at the farm. While they talked, two men in a white truck loaded with spray equipment and jugs of pesticide pulled up and began suiting up to spray the chicken house for bed bugs.

"This is my first time to encounter bed bugs in one of our houses," Dr. Anniston said, "but I spoke with some of the other corporate vets and found out it's happening more and more lately."

She turned her attention to MJ and Crawley. "And we really appreciate you getting us headed in the right direction as to controlling the pests. We found a company with a special license for agriculture operations. I'm confident this treatment will take care of it."

"Ain't gonna work," Crawley said flatly. "Too many places for the bug to hide."

Dr. Anniston's eyebrows went up. "I think what he's trying to say is that bed bugs are very difficult pests to control," MJ intervened hastily. "It might not be quite as simple as you think."

After an awkward silence, Dr. Anniston turned toward the men loading up their spraying equipment. "Let's see what happens."

A week later, there was a safety meeting at the Peace-of-Mind headquarters. "Have you heard anything from the chicken people?" Jack asked Crawley during the meeting. "Did their spraying get rid of the bed bugs?"

"The corporate woman claims they're gone, but Mr. Johnson thinks they's just as bad as before."

"Maybe corporate just doesn't want to face the ugly truth," MJ offered. "Should we go back out there and look around?"

Jack paused. "No, I guess not. Not unless they invite us. I had once thought this was an opportunity to expand our business — maybe even try for that special license myself — but now I'm not so sure."

"Maybe give it another week or so and we'll reassess?" MJ asked.

"I say wait until the birds are sold and then check the place," Crawley offered. "That's the only way to know for sure if the spraying worked."

Four months later, the chickens at the Johnson farm were sold to a soup company, so Crawley decided to check out the empty house. His curiosity was piqued; he couldn't stand not knowing what all those millions of bugs would do now that the chickens were gone. Would they crawl around inside the place, frantically looking for their animal hosts, or just hunker down and wait for a new set of laying hens? He remembered he had read somewhere that bed bugs don't actively disperse much, they were mostly just passively transferred around in personal belongings like suitcases, boxes, bags and things like that.

It was almost 9 p.m. by the time he made the drive into the country to check the poultry house. The moon above was only a tiny crescent, and since there were no streetlights, the farm lay eerily dark. When Crawley turned into the driveway at the facility, his headlights illuminated the outside walls and grounds surrounding the poultry house. He was horrified at what he saw!

"Oh, my gosh! It can't be!"

Crawley frantically fumbled for the gear stick and threw the truck into reverse as quickly as he could, speeding away. There was no way he was going to get near that!

He had a difficult time getting the image out of his mind.

The next morning, MJ found Crawley sitting in the office's examination room, staring out the window, deep in thought. He seemed nervous and fidgety, like something was bothering him.

"Hey Crawley, I've been looking for you." She pulled up a chair and eased down beside him. "I was wondering how things worked out with the bed bugs at the Johnson chicken farm."

"I've been readin' up on bed bugs." He paused, not meeting her eyes. "Oh MJ, you just don't know what I saw …"

"What? What's wrong? Are you all right?"

"Oh MJ …"

Then Jack entered the room, and MJ stood up, straightening her uniform. "Hi Jack, Crawley was trying to tell me about the bed bug treatment at the Johnson farm."

Jack pulled up a chair and straddled it. "That's what I want to know, too, so I can plan your schedules. Are we totally done out there or not?" He looked down. "Not that we did actually did anything but hook them up with somebody else. Should we make contact with the veterinarian again?"

Crawley stood up and began nervously pacing the floor. Jack watched him from the chair, while MJ stood back, arms across her chest. She didn't like Jack pressuring him like that.

"What?" Jack said to Crawley. "It couldn't be that bad. You're acting like a school kid in the principal's office."

"It was awful. Positively awful." His big eyes bounced around behind his glasses.

Jack stood up. "Did you accidentally burn the chicken house down or something?"

"Jack, don't do him like that," MJ chided. "Give him a chance to speak."

Crawley stopped pacing and turned toward them. His face showed both fear and confusion. "I went out there last night to check on things after the birds were sold." He stopped short.

"And?" Jack was losing patience.

"Well, bed bugs was coming out of the poultry house by the millions. In *waves,* just waves and waves of them coming out of the ceiling and walls, and crawling down the outer walls, and then out across the yard."

That stopped Jack cold. MJ's eyes were stark ovals by now.

"It was like a horror movie. The bugs were moving across the grass like a mighty army outward in all directions from the chicken house."

"Where? Where were they headed?" Jack asked.

"Don't know." Crawley shrugged. "Out across the land toward those little houses on the east side."

"You mean where the migrant workers live?"

"Yup. And I can't stand to think about it. Some of 'em have little kids."

Jack looked at MJ. "Did you know they can do that? I mean, disperse across land to another location?"

"Never heard of it, but I'm with Crawley. What'll happen if they make it to those houses? It's my understanding that two of the families are relocating to new farms out-of-state next week."

"Uh oh," Crawley said.

"Uh oh, indeed," Jack said.

"Lord help us all," MJ said solemnly.

CHAPTER 6

Crawley and the Bugs at Mrs. Welch's House

MJ O'Donnell knew she had to do *something.* Crawley was in a funk. The eccentric pest control technician had been feeling dejected after a couple of recent situations at work had left him feeling under-appreciated. So, during lunch hour at the Peace-of-Mind Pest Services headquarters, she searched for him to cheer him up.

When she couldn't find him in his office or in the bug examination room, MJ marched to the front office to ask Margie, the office manager, about it.

"Are you sure Crawley's not out servicing an account right now? I can't find him."

"I sincerely doubt it, as slow as he's been lately." Margie scowled, then ran her finger down a handwritten sheet of paper taped to the wall beside her. "Nope. Looks like his next scheduled appointment isn't until 2 p.m. He could be out running errands during lunch, you know."

"He's not slow, Margie. He's thorough — and there's a difference." MJ didn't appreciate Margie slamming her friend. Sure, Crawley was a bit socially off and had a difficult time sticking to schedules, but he was the most knowledgeable technician in the company. "He's really good, Margie. Cut him some slack." She turned to go. "I'll check if his truck's outside."

Outside, the June sunshine felt good on her face as she made her way across the parking lot. She spotted Crawley's truck and noticed what appeared to be the form of a man inside.

Uh oh. Hope he's not even more depressed.

MJ tapped the glass on the driver's side door. "Crawley? You all right in there?"

He rolled down the window and pulled ear buds out of his ears. His big eyes looked sad behind his thick glasses, but he didn't maintain eye contact for more than just a few seconds. "Yeah, I'm fine. Just listening to one of them pest control podcasts. Did you know flesh flies have four bristles on their notopleuron, and blow flies have only two or three? You can use that one little fact to tell them apart."

MJ looked him over closely and her heart went out to him. He was probably just saying all that to shift attention away from what was bothering him. The guy was really sweet and had indeed been mistreated lately. She figured he couldn't help it if he came across a little strange sometimes.

"Hey, I was wondering if you'd go with me to see Daisy Welch," she said. "Remember me asking you about her situation a while back? I could use your help."

He huffed and looked down, fiddling with his phone. "I'm afraid she's just one of them delusions of parasitosis folks like we saw a couple of months ago. The bug problem's probably all up in her head. There may not be much we can do."

"But we don't know that for sure. She could have a real bug problem. I'd still like for you to come look at it."

After what seemed like forever, he looked up. "Mmm. I guess I could go out there with you as long as I get to my scheduled stop by two o'clock." He paused. "But you'll see. Them DOP people'll drive you crazy and there's probably no bugs involved at all."

"Still, we've got to try. You don't know how much I appreciate this, Crawley. You want to follow me out there?"

"Yeah, I reckon I could do that."

Mrs. Welch lived in a one-story, ranch-style home built in the 1970s, complete with red brick walls, traditional white trim, and a two-car garage. Shrubbery surrounding the home was head-high and untrimmed. On the way walking up the driveway to her house, Crawley seemed to come alive, lecturing about delusions of parasitosis. "You watch, MJ. I've seen this a hun'rd times. She'll have a bunch of samples saved up for us in little vials or pill bottles. And she'll show us her so-called bites on her body, which will be mostly on her left side if she's right-handed."

"Because she's scratching herself, making the so-called bite marks?"

"Yep, that's right." Crawley's eyes danced with excitement. He seemed thrilled to describe the emotional disorder which was the bane of pest management technicians nationwide. "And then, she'll say the bugs are found everywhere, and not just one room. I knew one woman who said they followed her in a cloud everywhere, even to church."

"C'mon, Crawley, be nice," MJ chuckled as she knocked on the front door. "Remember, she's our customer."

Just then a scrawny dog rounded the corner of the house. It cautiously approached them, with its tail between its hind legs.

"Aww, look Crawley. Poor thing. I wonder if this is her dog."

Crawley bent over, running his hands gingerly over the dog's body. "It's OK, little dog, I'm just checking you over."

"Checking him over for what?"

"Ticks, mostly . . ." Soon Crawley had the dog lying on its back, legs up in the air, happily soaking up the free love. Crawley nudged his glasses up his nose to examine the animal's belly area more closely. "And fleas."

The door creaked open, and a very frail and wobbly little white-haired woman appeared. At once, Crawley could tell she was not well. *It's DOP for sure.*

"Mrs. Welch, how are you this fine day?" MJ bubbled, trying to appear upbeat.

"About as well as can be expected, I guess." Mrs. Welch managed a weak smile. "I don't know how much longer I can put up with these bugs. They're biting and driving me crazy."

"Here, Mrs. Welch," MJ waved toward Crawley, "I want you to meet one of our technicians, Crawley McPherson. He's the best we've got. Really smart and loves bugs. If he doesn't know a particular factoid about bugs . . . well . . . it's just not known."

Crawley extended a hand. "I don't know about all that, ma'am, but I can help investigate your bug problem if you want me to."

"I'd like that very much."

"First, let me ask, is this your dog?" He pointed to the mutt, which was now standing next to MJ.

"Yes. Why do you ask?"

"Ever seen any fleas on him?"

"It's a she."

"She then. Ever noticed any fleas?"

"No, but my eyesight's not what it used to be."

"Mmm." Crawley looked past her into the house. "Ma'am, can I ask, where're the bugs worse at?"

Mrs. Welch seemed taken aback at his awkward wording. "What do you mean?"

"Where are they worser? Like what room has 'em the most?"

"Well, I've found that they're worse when I'm sleeping on the couch in the living room. Seems like I've been doing that a lot lately."

"You mean they're not everywhere in your house?"

"No, I don't guess." Her eyes got big. "Is that bad? Are they supposed to be?"

Crawley shook his head. "Where's your bites at? I mean, which arms or legs?"

"Oh, we can't examine you, ma'am," MJ interjected. "We aren't doctors."

"I didn't mean it thata' way," Crawley backtracked. "You can just tell us about your bites. We don't have to see them."

The little lady appeared totally befuddled now. "I have lots of bites, but I've never thought about where they're located. They're just . . . uh . . . everywhere, I guess."

"Mmm."

"What about samples?" MJ took over. "Have you collected any of the bugs for us to look at?"

"No, can't catch them. I'm pretty sure they're invisible. I read on the internet they might be no-see-ums."

"Uh oh," Crawley blurted out.

Mrs. Welch's face was becoming ashen. "What do you mean, 'uh oh?' Is something wrong?"

Crawley squirmed. "No, I didn't mean nothing like that. It's about you sayin' you ain't got no samples for us."

MJ intervened. "We can continue this discussion later. Don't you think we should get down to business? May we look around?"

"Of course!" Mrs. Welch waved her thin arm back toward the inside of the house. "By all means, go ahead."

Crawley made a beeline for the living room. "Where're you going?" MJ hollered after him.

"To examine that couch."

"Okay, I'll check the bedrooms. Call me if you find anything."

In no time, Crawley was like a bulldog going after a bone, down on his hands and knees looking all over, around, and even inside the couch. Cushions flew everywhere. He took a small vial of alcohol from his pocket and began wetting his finger with it, rubbing it along the frame and cushions, and then dabbing the finger back in the vial to remove any attached bugs.

If there's any mites or tiny insects here, I'll get 'em in this alcohol.

Mrs. Welch wobbled into the room, reaching out for the walls and furniture to steady herself as she walked along. "Finding anything, young man?"

"Naw, not so far." He sat back, pushing his glasses up his nose. "Is this the couch you said you've been sleeping on?"

"Yes."

"Is it always pushed up against the outside wall and window like this?"

"Why, yes. Does that matter?" She leaned over like she was examining the top edge of the couch. "Have you found any lice or bed bugs on this thing?"

"Of course not," he huffed. "I ain't found nothing like that. But, I'm taking some samples with this alcohol so I can examine it later for mites."

"Can you see mites? It scares me that they might be living in here and I can't see them."

"Mites ain't invisible, but they're sure 'nough hard to see. They're about the size of a grain of sand."

The woman seemed worried. "Could it be no-see-ums?"

"Naw, you can see a no-see-um. They're not invisible. Besides, they breed outdoors along the edges of ponds, lakes, and salt marshes. They don't live inside houses."

Crawley got up and replaced the couch cushions. "I gotta inspect the other rooms and then look around outside."

"Yes, please do," she pleaded. "I really need some help."

Crawley walked out of the room. *It's gotta be the DOP.*

While he was inspecting the kitchen, MJ showed up. She leaned close to him in order to whisper. "You still think it's DOP?"

His pulse quickened. "Uh, not sure." Whenever MJ was anywhere near him, he had a difficult time concentrating. "Probably is the DOP, but some things don't add up."

"Find anything?"

"No, but I took some dust samples in alcohol from the couch. I'll look at 'em after I get done with my next customer."

MJ checked her watch. "You about to leave?"

He looked at the floor. "Yeah, Jack's been fussing at me about not doing enough stops lately, and I'm getting tired of it." A long pause ensued. "But I gotta look outside here first before I leave."

"C'mon, Crawley, you're not the only one he fusses at. He's all right. He's just trying to increase the company's efficiency."

"Maybe . . . but it still bothers me. Can't he just leave me alone to do my job?"

"Then tell him that. Stick up for yourself."

He turned to go. "I'm going outside."

"Okay then, see you back at the office. We can talk more there."

Once in the yard, Crawley was surprised to find that the big window where the couch was located was almost totally obscured from the outside by a large privet hedge. He fought his way through the thick, twisted limbs to examine the windowsill, and was shocked to see what looked like bird seed scattered about on it.

"What the heck?" he said aloud. "How did these seeds get here?"

Then he carefully pushed the shrubbery limbs back further so he could better examine the entire window. There was clearly a separation between the bricks and the edge of the window. "Uh oh. That would let pests go inside the walls." His mind ran wild with possibilities. *This here requires a closer inspection.*

He checked his watch — 1:45 p.m. He knew he had to get on to his next service stop.

It was 4:30 p.m. before Crawley got back to the office. He scurried past Margie in the front office, headed toward the bug examination room.

"Hey Crawley," she hollered after him. "Jack's looking for you."

Oh brother. That can't be good.

Crawley made his way to the bug room. Jack would have to wait. Something about the Welch account didn't make sense, and he was eager to examine the samples he had taken there today. Then he would have something to report to MJ. As much as he didn't want to admit it, there really could be a pest problem in Mrs. Welch's house. Maybe these samples would shed light on the situation.

He carefully poured the contents of his alcohol vial into a small petri dish and began the examination using a dissecting microscope. At first, everything looked clear, but under higher magnification, the liquid was actually full of dust, debris, lint and all sorts of tiny fibers. Crawley deliberately slowed down scanning the dish, paying careful attention to the contents floating in the alcohol. He knew mites could be hidden among the dust and debris.

After 15 minutes, he pushed his chair back and stretched his neck. This was like looking for a needle in a haystack. Mites were so tiny he would need to examine the contents in the petri dish again. And perhaps a third time. Pest control often required tedious detective work and lots of time.

Can't give up.

Just then, Jack popped in the doorway. "Oh, there you are. I've been looking everywhere for you."

Crawley eased back up to the microscope and started looking through the objectives again. "I've got to finish looking at these samples from the Welch account."

Jack wouldn't be deterred, pulling up a chair right beside Crawley. "We need to talk."

Crawley sat back, trying his best to be respectful. "Yes, sir."

"Crawley, as you and I have discussed several times lately, this company has certain targets for number of stops for each technician per day, and that should be between about 11 and 15 service stops a day."

"But that's for quarterly outside perimeter spraying," Crawley said. "Most times for me though, I have to investigate things." He paused. "And uh, help folks with their bug infestations. That's what I do."

"Yes, I realize first-time customers require more time, and maybe also when someone has a particular problem indoors, but that's not what I'm talking about. I'm telling you that your numbers are consistently low. Way too low."

Crawley was taken aback. "Do y'all keep up with things like that? I don't pay no mind to it. I just try to solve peoples' bug problems."

"Yes, in fact we do keep stats on each technician. That's what any good owner or manager does."

During the awkward impasse over the next few moments, Crawley's throat became so dry he could barely speak. "What do you want me to do?" he squeaked.

"I really appreciate you being conscientious and trying so hard to help folks, but please try to reduce the amount of time you spend at each place," Jack said. "Let's set a goal to make 10 stops a day, and do our best to make it happen. If you can get it up to 10, I'll let you slide for awhile, then maybe we can increase it. But if not, I'm going to have to ride with you for a few days to see what the problem is and how we might make adjustments. Are we clear on that?"

Make adjustments? "Yes, sir."

Jack stood up, patted him on the back and disappeared out the door.

Crawley resumed examining the sample and refused to give up until he was absolutely sure there were no mites or insects in it. He got up to leave and checked his watch — 6:30 p.m.

"I'll have to go back out there tomorrow and get more samples, whether Jack likes it or not," he told himself.

The next morning Crawley was at Mrs. Welch's front door at 7 a.m. sharp. Surely, she would be up. Since he always got up early, he figured all people should do likewise. Crawley had on his service belt and several vials of alcohol stuffed in his pockets.

The elderly woman cracked open the door and peeped her gray head out. "Yeess?"

"Mrs. Welch, it's me, Crawley, the bug man. I'm sorry to bother you so early, but I was hoping you'd let me take some more samples from that couch of your'n. Would that be all right?"

She welcomed him inside. "Why yes, if you think it's necessary."

Crawley noticed fresh bloody scabs on the woman's arms and neck. "Are the bugs still biting you?"

"Oh yes, it's awful. Positively awful. I'm miserable."

"Did you sleep on that couch again last night?"

"Yes."

"Why you keep doin' that, if they're biting you there?"

She seemed embarrassed. "It's got special meaning to me. That's all I can say. My husband passed away a few months ago."

Crawley had no idea how to respond. "Can I get started collectin'? I need to get on with my regular pest control service stops right away."

In no time, he was rooting around in the floor beside the couch, taking dust samples in and under the thing. Mrs. Welch wobbled up beside him, studying his every move.

"Seeing anything?" she asked.

Crawley sat up, leaning back, his hands planted on the carpeted floor behind him.

"Mrs. Welch, could I ask you a question?"

"Yes."

"Yesterday, when I was examining right outside there," he nodded toward the window, "I saw bird seed on the windowsill. Did you put it there?"

Her eyebrows went up. "Yes I did, is that bad?"

"Why would you be a'doing that?"

"To feed the birds. When my husband was alive, he watched birds in the hedge out there."

"But the couch is facing the wrong way for that."

"Didn't used to be." She waved a bony arm. "It was angled in that direction where he could see outside."

Crawley suddenly felt a slight tingling or crawling sensation on his hands, which had been on the carpeted floor. He sat up and examined them carefully, like a jeweler might examine a diamond. Sure enough, what appeared to be freckles on his right hand were moving!

"Uh oh."

"What's wrong?"

Crawley scrambled for an alcohol vial and quickly transferred a couple of the tiny brown mites into the liquid. He then turned on his all-fours and began examining the baseboard under the window. He found more mites.

Crawley stood up and tapped on the wall beside the window. "This here's your problem, Mrs. Welch. I'll bet you anything there's a bird nest in this wall. You were calling them up by feeding birds out there and they entered the wall through cracks outside and made nests. And now you have bird mites."

"Oh my, can you spray them? Do I have to get rid of my couch?"

Crawley placed his hands on his service belt like a gunslinger and smiled a big toothy grin. "No need to throw out the couch. Don't you worry one bit. I'll get 'em."

Just then, his phone rang. It was MJ. He was excited to hear her voice.

"Hello?"

"Crawley, where in the world are you?" she sounded exasperated. "Margie said you never came in this morning to get more chemicals and turn in yesterday's tickets. Don't you know Jack's gonna be mad at you for not showing up?"

"I'm at Mrs. Welch's place. I found the mites! I guarantee they're bird mites living in the wall and in the couch. I'm about to spray the mess outta them."

"Why didn't you tell me? I could've gone out there with you. You don't have to do my accounts."

"I just got to thinking about it last night, MJ, and got carried away. You know I don't sleep too good. I knew it had to be a bird nest or something."

She seemed to calm down. "What all are you going to have to do? How long will it take?'

"I've gotta treat the floor and couch, then cut a hole in the drywall to clean out the nesting area. Then spray real good. Then I gotta go outside and seal up that big crack."

"That'll take hours, Crawley! What about your other stops today?"

"Ain't got time to talk, MJ. Gotta kill bugs!"

"I'll try to cover for you with Jack —"

Crawley punched the "end call" button. Jack would just have to understand. This was what he was born to do. And he was going to do it, no matter the consequences.

CHAPTER 7

Crawley and the Ant Problem

At 10 a.m., Jack Blackwell, owner of Peace-of-Mind Pest Services, punched Crawley's number on his cell phone.

"Heelloo?"

"Crawley, I want you go to that personal care home on Taylor Road today. I think the name of it is Heavenly Hope House. I've been getting reports from some of the patients' families that they've got an ant problem."

"Yeah, I can do that, but ain't that Paul Bono's account?"

"Yes, but he's had them on a green program that doesn't seem to be working. I want you to go look-see."

"Mmm."

"This is serious, Crawley. Do you remember that case last summer in Texas? Some lady in a nursing home was attacked by ants, then the family sued the mess out of both the nursing home and the pest control company. The judgment was millions of dollars. When it comes to health-related issues, I can't take any chances, so go check it out for me."

"I don't want Paul mad at me."

"Don't worry, I've already talked to him. Besides, he won't be angry. I'm the one who gave him permission to put them on a green protocol. You just make plans to get out there ASAP. And don't be wasting time."

"Yes, sir."

Crawley headed to the office for a quick lunch and to pick up more chemicals for his 1 p.m. appointment. He figured he could swing by Heavenly Hope House after that. On the way inside the pest control shop, he pretended to be on his phone to avoid facing the office manager, Margie. He didn't want to have to justify where he had been or what he had been doing all morning. That woman was just plain nosy.

Margie looked him over as he walked by, but didn't say anything. But when he passed MJ O'Donnell's office, MJ hollered at him, "Hey Crawley, come in here a minute."

His heart skipped a beat. *Why would MJ want to talk to me?*

"Have a seat." She pointed at the chair in front of her desk. "I've been meaning to ask if you're going to the national pest control meeting. I think Jack'll let us go since it's in late October, the off-season. He might even pay part of it. Maybe we could ride together."

Crawley was literally shivering by now. The thought of riding in a car on a trip with MJ — no matter how close or far — unnerved him. He could feel his face flushing so he looked down momentarily, rubbing his palms on his thighs. "Uh, I guess. Yes, that would be wonderful. I mean, wonderful to get to attend such high-powered educational sessions."

When he noticed her studying him, he quickly looked away again, hoping she couldn't see what he was thinking. After a few more awkward moments, MJ stood up. "Come on, let's go to the break room. I'll buy you a Coke.

"Yeah, sure. Okay." Crawley tried his best to act normal, as if there was a such a thing for him. He nudged his glasses up his nose and followed her to the break room. *Please don't embarrass yourself, Crawley. Please.*

By the time he arrived at Heavenly Hope House, Crawley's self-confidence had started to return. The thing at lunch with MJ had rattled him. He jumped out of the truck, straightened his uniform, and headed inside. He knew he wasn't much to look at, but perhaps his knowledge of bugs could make up for that.

From the outside, in the blazing July sunlight, the personal care home appeared no different from a regular three or four bedroom ranch-style house. He guessed they had converted a single family dwelling into a personal care home. The only way one might know it was a personal care home from the outside was the line of huge security lights mounted all around the eaves of the house.

"I guess they don't want them people getting loose," he muttered.

Just inside the house was a big common room, with lots of chairs and a TV. A small check-in station was located just inside the front door, where a receptionist asked sharply, "May I help you?"

"Uh, I'm here to do a pest inspection."

What little smile she had previously displayed instantly evaporated. "I thought y'all just did an inspection last week. Why would you need to do it again so soon?"

"I was told to come look at your ant problem, ma'am. It won't take long."

The woman suddenly seemed agitated. "Who told you we had an ant problem? We're not aware of any ant incidents with the patients."

Even Crawley could see through that. "Nobody said nothin' about no incidents. I'm just looking around for ants."

"OK." She picked up the phone. "But I'm going to let Ms. Conway, the owner, know you're here. But I can tell you right now, she wouldn't want you spraying around the place. The fumes can be highly toxic to our patients."

"That's not true. Pesticides are safe when used rightly."

"Well, you can look around, but please don't start dousing the place with chemicals without permission from Ms. Conway. It's my understanding the other pest man from your company has us on a non-toxic treatment schedule."

"If it's non-toxic, then how's it killing anything?" Crawley popped off. "By definition, any pesticide is toxic. Pest-ti-*cide* means 'kills pests.'"

She looked him over condescendingly. "Of course, you wouldn't understand."

Crawley bit his lip to keep from saying more. Then there was the voice in his head — MJ's. *Be patient, Crawley. Remember, these are our customers.*

He turned to begin his inspection. His initial walk-through of the home revealed six patient rooms and three bathrooms in the back part of the house. Up front were the common room and kitchen. Crawley examined each room carefully for signs of ant infestation, particularly fire ants. He knew he'd need to check the outside perimeter of the house as well.

In the third bedroom, a slight, elderly man was sitting in a recliner beside his bed watching TV. He seemed to be having a difficult time eating an individual serving-sized chocolate pudding. He had a distant look in his eyes.

"You want some of my C-rations, soldier?" The man glanced out the window. "The Viet Cong are coming. We've got to hurry and get over to that next ridge."

Crawley had seen dementia before in personal care and nursing home patients, but he glanced out the window just to make sure. He certainly didn't want to meet up with the Viet Cong. "No, I've done eaten. I'm just the pest man doing an inspection. You had any problems with bugs in here?"

The man gave him a blank look, nodded, then shook his head.

Crawley noticed a lone ant crawling along the baseboard and ran over to investigate. He got down on his knees and collected the specimen in a small vial of alcohol. He looked around for other ants, then went over to the recliner to show it to the man. "You been seeing any of these ants in here?"

Blank look again, then he spoke. "Yes, lots of men crawling over the hill, coming toward us."

Crawley had no idea how to respond. He tried to orient himself to the outside wall and then headed outside.

When he got outside the building, and specifically, outside the room where the confused patient was, he immediately noticed two large fire ant mounds situated right next to the house foundation.

Crawley whistled. "That's not good."

He worked his way around the rest of the house perimeter, counting fire ant mounds next to the foundation. "Six!" he exclaimed. He pulled out his cell phone and called Jack to report the fire ant mounds around the personal care home.

Upon hearing the report, Jack became concerned. "What do you think, Crawley? Is it that the green products are just flat not working? You think Paul's been appropriately applying them?"

"I wouldn't say that. These anti-pesticide people are limiting him from spraying, even with green products. He's probably doing the best he can, just caught between a rock and a hard place."

"Well, he needs to do his job. If they don't want our services, we can just walk away from it. And then see how they like that."

"Maybe it won't come to that," Crawley said. "But one thing, I'm thinking I don't need to leave here today without treating these mounds up against the foundation. I think I'll drench 'em, and then also, maybe spray the perimeter about 25 feet out from the foundation all the way around the house."

"She's not going to like it," Jack said. "But maybe since it's outside only, she'll allow it. Either way, we've got to do it. We can't have any of the patients getting stung by ants."

"Oh," Crawley continued, "and maybe you could ask Paul to come by here tomorrow to re-inspect inside the rooms and treat where needed."

"Done."

As soon as Jack hung up, Crawley went and got in his truck and drove around to the back yard of the house.

Fortunately, it had been an unusually dry July, and he was able to drive through the grass right up to the spot outside the little old man's room. He got out and began unrolling the hose from the power sprayer mounted in the truck bed. He mixed the pesticide and got ready to begin spraying the foundation wall and portions of the yard.

"*What* are you doing, young man?" a firm voice called out from behind him.

Crawley whirled around. A sixtyish, silver-haired woman was standing there, hands on her hips.

"I *said*, what are you doing?"

"Spraying for fire ants, ma'am. I'm from the pest control company."

"Oh, you're most certainly not going to do that. That stuff is nerve poison."

"Maybe to the bugs, it's a nerve poison," Crawley said, fighting the urge to giggle.

"Don't argue with me. I insist you stop immediately."

Crawley knew better than to disagree with a customer. "Okay, I'll stop." He switched off the engine of the sprayer and started rolling the hose back on the rack. "But may I ask why you don't want me to spray these fire ants?"

"Just as I told the other man from your company, I don't mind you treating a little inside the house, but outdoors, we don't want to kill any little creatures."

"But these ants can go indoors and attack the patients. Don't you care about that?"

She crossed her arms tightly across her chest. "As I said, you can put out a limited amount of your products inside, but that's all. We've got to be good stewards, you know."

He could see it was useless to argue. He would need to call Jack.

The next morning, Crawley was summoned by Jack to discuss the situation. Paul was already in Jack's office when he arrived.

Jack had a strained look on his face. "Thanks for coming, Crawley. Have a seat."

Crawley took a seat next to Paul, who was nervously sipping a cup of coffee out of white foam cup.

"I told Paul what happened yesterday out at the personal care home." He stopped and folded his hands like a preacher. "And I thought it would be good for us to discuss the situation face-to-face. We need a plan of action."

"She wouldn't let me spray the mounds and a 25-foot perimeter in the yard," Crawley started. "But I wasn't about to make no big fuss."

Jack turned his attention to Paul. "Has this ever happened before?"

Paul twisted uncomfortably in his chair. "Yes, to be honest, Ms. Conway will barely let me use anything during my regular pest service."

"Why didn't you tell me? I could have called and tried to explain our IPM program to her."

"I guess I thought I could work around her and still get the job done."

"I need to know... have you been treating outside the structure for fire ants?"

Paul hesitated. "Well no, she insisted not to. Said they were part of nature."

Jack leaned back. "We can't let this go on. If someone gets attacked, we're the ones on the hook. She'll deny telling you not to spray." He picked up the phone and dialed the personal care home.

"Hello, this is Jack Blackwell from Peace-of-Mind Pest Services. Is Ms. Conway in?"

Once connected to her office, Jack listened intently and didn't say anything for what seemed to be an eternity. Crawley had no idea what the person on the other end of the line was saying, but all of a sudden the look on Jack's face said it all. He slammed the phone down and jumped up.

"C'mon, we've got to go out there. One of the patients has been stung by fire ants!"

"Who?" Crawley asked. "Was it that little old man who was a veteran?"

"How on earth would I know?" Jack snapped. "The woman just said someone got attacked and that the paramedics were there."

As they rushed down the hall toward the front door, Crawley quickly stuck his head in MJ's door. "Can you go with us to a personal care home? We've got big trouble."

She rose from her chair with a troubled look. "Why would y'all need me?"

"I guess it's me needing you, MJ. This is serious."

"Sure," she said, reaching for her purse. "We can go in my truck. It's parked right outside the door. I just stopped by for a few minutes to update my spreadsheet."

Soon they zipped their way out of the parking lot and onto the main road. They spotted Jack's truck about a quarter mile ahead.

"Which personal care home is it?" she asked.

"The one out on Taylor Road."

"I think I've been there before, but it was a few years back," MJ replied. "Tell me what happened."

"It's bad." Crawley shook his head. "It's real bad." He then relayed to her the events of the last couple of days. "They've called an ambulance," he said when finished. "That's all we know."

"Did they ever put in writing that they didn't want spraying?"

"What?"

"Specifically, is there anything *written* that they didn't want you to treat for ants according to our protocol? Are there any e-mails or texts or anything like that?"

"Well no, I don't guess."

MJ whipped into the parking lot, pulling up beside Jack Blackwell. "Then they're gonna deny ever saying it, you watch and see," she said, grimly.

They jumped out of the truck and followed Jack and Paul toward the entrance of the personal care home. A fire truck was parked just outside the front door with its lights flashing, as was an ambulance with its back doors open. The stretcher was missing and there were no signs of any paramedics.

Jack swung open the front door of the building and waved them inside. "Come on, let's see how bad this is." He paused, looking at Crawley. "And let me do the talking. This'll likely turn into a lawsuit."

There was no one at the front desk as they made their way through the big common room and down the hall toward the patient rooms. Outside the third bedroom, a small crowd had gathered. Paramedics and firefighters were going in and out of the room, while several staff members and other adults were standing nearby. A few of the people were openly weeping.

"Oh no, it *is* the little veteran man!" Crawley cried out. "I hope he's gonna be all right."

Jack shot him a stern look as they eased up to the crowd.

Ms. Conway strode purposefully toward Jack. She had a grave look on her face.

"I'm glad to see you people," she said, loud enough for everybody to hear. "There's been a fire ant stinging incident, and you might be needed to answer questions. The state health inspectors and possibly even the police may want to speak to you."

"Why would the police want to speak to us?" Jack bristled.

"I'm sorry to say Mr. Turnage has passed," Ms. Conway said crisply. "There'll be a thorough investigation, just to make sure there was no foul play. We expect everyone involved to cooperate fully."

Just then, an older woman and what appeared to be her grown daughter edged their way through the crowd and confronted Ms. Conway. The older woman's eyes bulged and her cheeks were bright red. "You're responsible for my husband's death!" she screamed. "When we got here, we found him with fire ants all over him, coming out of his mouth, ears and nose. Thousands of them. They stung him to death. You did it! You neglected him! I want you to know, we're holding you personally responsible."

"Oh no," Ms. Conway calmly responded, turning toward Jack and the others from Peace-of-Mind Pest Services. "Heavenly Hope House isn't responsible. We don't know anything about pests and their control. That's why we hired the best pest control company in town — to protect our patients from ants, bugs, and all kinds of things like that. If one of the patients was attacked by bugs, it's … uh … the pest people's fault, not ours."

Jack backed up, shocked at the accusation. Paul slipped behind Jack, as if hiding. MJ took Crawley's arm protectively.

"That there's not true!" Crawley blurted out. "You've been telling Paul not to treat for pests for months. And you know it."

"I never did any such thing! We would never attempt to second-guess your pest management procedures. It's our official policy to trust your expertise in these matters."

Crawley's eyes were huge ovals by now behind his glasses. His face was beet red. He tried to lunge forward toward Ms.

Conway, but MJ pulled him back. "You told me just yesterday not to spray for the fire ants."

Ms. Conway feigned surprise. "Why, I never said —"

Jack intervened, putting himself between Crawley and Ms. Conway. "C'mon guys, we're not going to do this. Not here, not now. Let's go."

All the way out of the building they could hear Mr. Turnage's wife and daughter hollering after them about how they killed their husband and father.

Once outside in the parking lot, Jack turned, gathered his team together, and spoke softy to them, making sure no one else could hear him. "This is dead serious, and a matter for our insurance company. These people are gonna sue us."

"What're we going to do?" Paul asked, ashen-faced. "She'll pin this on us."

Crawley was indignant. "I didn't have no idea she would act like it was all our fault. This is awful."

"It certainly is," MJ offered. "We're gonna be in trouble if we can't somehow prove she restricted us from spraying."

"We should've gotten it in writing or taped our conversations with her," Jack said with a sigh. "But we'll learn from it. You'll see. It'll make us better."

CHAPTER 8

Crawley and the Baffling Flea Infestation

Martha Mooney was trying her best to relax at home after a long day at work as an attorney, but she kept unconsciously scratching and clawing at her waist and legs. Finally, she realized what she was doing and looked down. What appeared to be bug bites of various sizes and stages covered her thighs. She raised her shirt, and the results were the same: Big red welts dotted her waist and stomach area. Some of them were beginning to bleed from her scratching.

"Where are these things coming from, Thomas? What's going on here?"

Her husband, sitting across the living room, lifted his head above his newspaper.

"It's August, dear," he said. "You probably just got mosquito bites from being out on the patio or by the pool. Maybe we should talk to the pest control people about installing one of those mosquito-misting systems around our house."

"These aren't mosquito bites. How could they be around my waist and under my shirt? If they're mosquitoes, wouldn't there be bites on my arms and hands?"

Martha looked around the opulently furnished room. "Do you think there could be some sort of insects or mites infesting this room? Maybe parasites?"

"Don't be silly. This house is almost brand new. Those bites have got to be coming from outdoors."

She shook her head. "Not so. I'm calling our pest control man tomorrow. Maybe he can do an inspection."

"You mean that goofy-acting guy?"

"Don't make fun of him. I understand he's the best pest control person they've got. Besides, I think he's got autism spectrum disorder."

Thomas snapped the paper open in front of him. "If he's the best, I'd sure hate to see their worst."

A security guard waved Crawley into the gated community where the Mooneys lived. He marveled at the big new houses, many of which were still under construction. He recalled how just one year ago the whole area was nothing but woods. He knew the place was too fancy for him. He couldn't even pay the insurance on these houses.

The Mooneys' house was at the edge of the subdivision, barely 100 feet from the tree line. Crawley pulled in the circular drive, gathered his things, and walked up some high steps to the front door. He thought it strange that the house was on a conventional foundation, instead of a slab.

Crawley noticed several security cameras in the eaves of the front porch, and fought the urge to make a face or do a little dance to shock whomever was monitoring them. *People this rich probably have a whole team of security officers watching the videos around the clock.*

He used the knocker on the massive oak door to announce his arrival instead of the doorbell. Presently, Thomas Mooney opened the door and waved him in.

"Come on in, Mr. McPherson, I'm glad you're here. My wife's been driving me crazy, claiming there's bugs in the house."

Crawley nudged his glasses back up his nose. "Ain't no bugs here. Too new. Probably something else."

Thomas looked at him, puzzled. "What do you mean by that?"

Crawley nervously ran a hand through his hair. "Uh, nothing. I was just … ah … thinking out loud. Where're the bugs at?"

Thomas paused. "I suppose in the living room. At least that's where we've been almost every time she's noticed the biting."

"Mmm."

"Come on, I'll show you."

Even though Crawley had been to the house before, he was still in awe of how expensive everything looked. It seemed like he was led through three foyers and an equal number of what looked like dining rooms just to get to the living room. The furniture looked like it came from one of those high-falutin' places, like Restoration Hardware. As he walked by one of the couches, he noticed a distinct and obvious leathery smell. Crawley had learned from being in rich peoples' homes that real leather furniture always smelled like real leather.

Martha Mooney was there waiting for them, sitting on a big, poufy cushion on the wide fireplace hearth.

"Hello, Mr. McPherson," she displayed a cautious smile. "We've definitely got a bug problem in here, and need you to fix it."

"How you know it's bugs?" he said flatly.

"Well, I've got bites all over my legs, waist and stomach. It's got to be bugs. What else could it be?"

"They're all sorts of things that can be like a bug bite. Fiberglass, allergic reactions, and things like that."

She shook her head. "No, it's an insect or a parasite. I'm convinced of it."

"Have you ever seen or caught one of 'em?"

"No. If I did, wouldn't I know what the problem is?"

Crawley looked around the room, instantly evaluating the place for any sort of insect harborage or breeding site. "You got any pets?"

"No." She seemed frustrated. "It's just us two living here, no other people, pets, ghosts, aliens, or anything. Can't you just please spray the place?"

"No ma'am. We don't spray inside a house without having a target organism identified."

"Then you better get started identifying, because I about had enough of this."

Crawley nodded and began examining the room carefully, starting with the baseboards, looking for any sign of insect activity.

Martha got up and followed him around, seemingly skeptical. "Maybe it's fleas?" she suggested.

"Oh Martha, you've suggested just about every insect on earth," Thomas said. "It's not fleas. The house is still new, and we don't have any pets."

Irritated, Martha plopped back down on her cushion on the hearth, and picked up a magazine.

Just then, Crawley had a thought. "I noticed this here house is on a conventional foundation."

"Yes, what does that have to do with anything?" demanded Thomas.

"Is it all sealed up? I mean, can an animal get up under there? Wild animals can have fleas on them — and you're mighty close to the woods. It could be raccoons or something bringing 'em up."

"Of course it's sealed up," Thomas said. "What do you think this is, a trailer park?"

What's wrong with a trailer park? Crawley didn't know how to respond, so he kept pressing on. "What about the chimney? Is it sealed up, too? Is there a screen on top?"

Thomas lowered his head, staring hard at Crawley. "Do you have any idea how much money houses cost in this neighborhood? Our builder would never halfway do something."

Crawley shook his head. He was out of ideas. "Well, I'm gonna look around inside some more and set out a few glue boards to see if I can catch anything. Then I'll check the outside foundation. And I might make a preventive perimeter application of pesticides out there for you. I can do that as part of your regular quarterly service contract."

"Whatever you think you need to do," Martha said, uncertainty in her voice.

"Well, I'll say this. If we don't catch anything on the sticky traps, and the biting continues, please call our office and we'll come back out," Crawley replied. "I might bring somebody with me next time to help me investigate. This sure is a strange case."

"I wish you'd fix this pest problem before we go on vacation next week," Martha said with a huff. "I can't wear my bathing suit at the beach with all these horrible bites on my body."

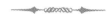

Two days later, Crawley spotted MJ in the break room at Peace-of-Mind Pest Services. He needed to speak to her about the mystery bugs at the Mooney residence. Despite Martha's claim about bugs biting her, Crawley's inspection had turned up nothing.

When MJ saw Crawley, she smiled. "Hey there, Crawley! Haven't seen you lately. How's it going?"

"Uh, OK, I guess. Just sorta tired."

"Tired?" She looked him over. "I know you spend a lot of time up here working late. You getting enough rest?"

He looked away. "I don't sleep much, MJ."

"Why?" Her face was filled with compassion.

Total silence. He wouldn't meet her eyes.

"Tell you what," she smiled. "I'm gonna text you every night for awhile to wish you a good night. You know, as friends. Would that help?"

"You don't have to do that." He squirmed. "Besides, it wouldn't work. You probably go to bed way before me."

"OK, then, I'll text you every morning for awhile and wish you a happy day!"

He appreciated her concern, but had no idea how to respond. "Uh OK, that'd be good."

She smiled. "Now, what else can I help you with?"

"I was hoping to talk to you about one of my customers."

MJ was startled. "You're asking *me* for pest control advice? It's usually the other way around."

"This one's got me stumped, MJ."

"C'mon over to the table. I'll get you a candy bar, then we can discuss your case."

No amount of sugar could calm Crawley's nerves around MJ. She was so beautiful. After several awkward stops and starts, he managed to explain the mysterious bug infestation to her. He hoped she would be able to make sense of his bumbling conversation. To his surprise, MJ listened attentively.

"So there you go, MJ," Crawley finally stopped. "There's something supposedly biting Ms. Mooney, but I can't find it out."

"No mosquitoes or seed ticks?"

"Nope."

"No mites, like at Mrs. Welch's house?"

He shook his head.

"What about fleas?"

"I thought about that, but I can't find none. I even placed a white handkerchief on the floor here and there, hoping to spot fleas. Nothing."

"You said the house is on a conventional foundation. Do you think a wild animal is getting up under the house? That could be causing a flea problem."

"I told you I checked for fleas and didn't see none."

"Maybe it's a spotty infestation and you didn't sample in the right places."

Crawley ignored that comment. "I found the door to the crawlspace under the house, but it was closed up tight."

"Doesn't mean it's always closed. Maybe you should go look again. I bet this is a flea problem."

"Mmm."

"What do you mean by that?"

"I was just thinking … the Mooneys told me they were going to be out of town on vacation next week. Maybe I could go investigate more thoroughly while they're gone."

"You can't go in someone's house without permission!"

Crawley grinned. "I didn't say nothing about going *inside*. I can call and ask them permission to walk around outside their house, looking for evidence of wild animals at various times of the day."

The following Wednesday, MJ was up early. She texted Crawley to wish him a happy day, just as she had done every day since their conversation the week before. This time, though, he didn't respond. But this was sometimes the case with him. She didn't mind — that was just the way he was.

MJ arrived at the office by 7 a.m., trying to catch up on paperwork and make a few calls to customers lining up her stops for the day. Quarterly perimeter treatments at residences didn't require calling the customer first, but indoor pest service did, and MJ still retained a few of those accounts.

Soon Margie showed up, turning on lights up and down the hall and bringing the building to life. She popped her head in MJ's office. "Hey MJ, you seen Crawley?"

"No, why?"

"He didn't show up at all yesterday afternoon, and I've been calling and leaving him messages. Jack wants him to look at a cockroach problem at the Garden of Eatin' Restaurant."

"He hasn't answered his calls?" *And he didn't respond to my text this morning,* MJ added silently, becoming worried.

Margie shook her head. "That little guy needs to be more responsible."

"Do you know what was his last stop yesterday?"

"Out east of town, near those gated communities on Winchester."

MJ's pulse quickened. That was where the Mooneys lived.

"If you see him this morning," Margie continued, "tell him to call me."

MJ rose from her desk, reaching for her keys. "Uh, yeah, sure."

She tried dialing Crawley's number as she made her way through the parking lot toward her truck. When he failed to answer, MJ left a message for him to call her. Then she recalled him saying he might do some investigating at the Mooney home while they were on vacation. What if he were hurt or injured?

When MJ drove up to the Mooney house, Crawley's truck was nowhere in sight. "Maybe he's not here after all," she thought. She put the gearshift in park and hopped out to take a quick look anyway.

MJ checked the front door. Surely, he wouldn't try to go inside while the Mooneys were away. She found the house locked and silent, so she went around to the back. The opening to the crawlspace under the house was ajar — and there were signs of disturbed dirt at the opening.

MJ leaned over, opened the door wide, and peered under the house. She spotted a Little Debbie's honey bun wrapper on the ground just inside the opening. *Crawley!*

MJ raised back up and looked around. Crawley had surely been under the house. But where was he now? His truck was gone. She quickly scanned the neighborhood and tree line behind the house. Then something caught her eye, far back in the woods. It was a spot of white. The more she examined it, the more the object began to look like the outline of a truck. Crawley's truck.

She turned back to the opening to the crawlspace, piecing together that he must have hidden his truck so he could investigate under the house the night before.

MJ got down on her knees and positioned herself at the opening of the crawlspace. "Crawley?" she hollered. "You under here?"

Silence.

"It's me, MJ. Are you back in there? I'm worried about you."

She was just about to turn to go, when she heard a muffled voice far back inside the cavernous crawlspace. "Uh, yeah ... I'm here."

"Come out here. I want to talk to you."

Presently, Crawley emerged from under the house, dirt all over his clothes and in his hair. He dragged behind him what appeared to be an old, beat-up sleeping bag. When he stood up, it was easy for MJ to read embarrassment, almost guilt, all over him.

"Whatcha doing under there, Crawley? I've been worried sick about you."

"Uh, just lookin' under here for wild animals that could be bringing up fleas or sump'n like that."

"How long have you been under there?"

He looked down and shrugged.

"That's a sleeping bag," she pointed. "You spent the night under there, didn't you?"

"OK ... so I did." He fell silent for a full minute.

MJ instinctively hugged him. "Don't scare me like that again. If you're going to do crazy stuff, please let me or someone else know." She backed off and looked him over.

"C'mon, I'll go with you to your truck, then let's go get some breakfast."

On the way to the truck, she asked about his night. "Did you see anything? Any fleas or animals?"

"Nope. Ain't nothing under there. Clean as a pin."

"Then what's biting Ms. Mooney?"

He shrugged again. "I'm stumped. Fresh out of ideas."

Two weeks later, about 4 p.m., MJ saw Crawley eating a Payday candy bar in the break room at the Peace-of-Mind headquarters. He looked somber, as if he'd lost his best friend.

She made a beeline toward him. "Hey, Crawley. What are you doing?"

"Just sittin' here." He looked down.

"You don't have any customers today?"

"That ain't the problem."

"Then what is?"

He took a big swig from his soda can. "I need to go see the Mooneys, but I'm not wanting to."

"Why, Crawley?" she asked with concern. "There's no reason to feel bad."

Crawley looked up at her and frowned. "But I can't figure out what's biting them. What am I going to say?"

She patted his shoulder. "C'mon, let's go. I'll go with you."

Crawley stood up, but his face was strained. "OK, I guess we should just go get it over with."

Thomas Mooney met them at the door. "Hello. What brings you two out here?"

"We wanted to speak with you and your wife about our progress on your insect infestation," MJ said.

"Or lack thereof, I suppose," Thomas replied curtly. "I'm beginning to think it's all in her head or that we need to change to a new pest control company."

MJ was surprised at his blunt reply, and knew she needed to try to protect Crawley. He would take that as a personal failure.

"Oh no, Crawley and I have been working on it," she said quickly. "We've got some new information to share with you."

Crawley's face twisted as if that was news to him.

Thomas waved them in and escorted them to the living room. Martha was perched on her fireplace hearth cushion, opening a stack of mail. "Oh, hi," she said, unenthusiastically.

"Ms. Mooney, we just wanted to come update you and your husband about what all we've been doing about your insect problem while y'all were out of town." MJ was doing her thing — trying to empathize with customer feelings — but truth be told, in this case she had no real news to report.

She took a breath to continue, despite having no idea where the conversation was headed. Then she noticed Crawley staring hard at Martha, who was scratching again.

"Stupid bugs," the woman interrupted MJ. "I wasn't having any new bites while we were gone. Now it's started back again."

Crawley eased over toward her, his eyes like huge ovals bouncing around behind his glasses. He reached out toward her — then touched the cushion she was sitting on.

Martha shot up from the cushion like a rocket. "I beg your pardon!" she roared.

Crawley leaned past her and stuck his head into the opening of the fireplace. He took out his handkerchief and spread it out in the opening of the fireplace. Then he slowly ran his hand along the inside of the fireplace itself. Presently, a huge grin spread across his face.

MJ had seen that look before. *He had solved the case!*

He picked up the handkerchief. "Lookey here. There's fleas on this thing. Probably cat fleas."

Thomas ran over. "How could that be? I've told you we don't have pets."

"Other animals can have cat fleas," Crawley told him. "The fleas are coming down out of the chimney, probably from a raccoon sleeping up in there. They do that, I've seen it before. And especially since you're right up at the edge of the woods."

"Martha does sit there a lot," Thomas said softly.

"But how could a raccoon get in our chimney?" Martha was flabbergasted. "That's ridiculous."

"From the top. They climb up there and think it's a hollow tree."

"But the chimney's capped."

"I bet not."

"Oh yes, it is," Thomas interjected, then less confidently added, "Or supposedly, it is."

"Look, we can do a spot treatment here right now, but first thing tomorrow, why don't you call your builder and ask him or her to send someone out to check the chimney cap?" MJ said. "If it's not properly in place, tell them to inspect the chimney to make sure there's no animals in there and then cap it off."

"Wow!" Thomas was stunned. He turned to Crawley. "How did you know?"

"It just came to me. I remembered that every time I've been here, Ms. Mooney was sittin' right there." He looked down. "It shouldn't have taken me that long to figure it out. I'm sorry."

"I told y'all we had some news about your insect infestation," MJ said lightly.

"But he just now figured it out ..." Thomas said, then laughed. "Oh, never mind."

CHAPTER 9

Crawley and the Mysterious Allergic Reaction

Marci Ainsworth woke up in the middle of the night, gasping for air. Her stomach cramped violently. *What's going on?* Her breathing became increasingly labored, accompanied by wheezing. She stood up from the bed; the room swirled. Marci reached for the wall to stabilize herself. She somehow found her way to the bathroom sink and looked in the mirror. Her eyes were swollen almost shut and her lips were turned inside out.

"I must be dying!" she thought.

She reached for her phone to call her sister, Donna, the only family she had in town. If she could only make the call before passing out!

By mid-morning the next day, Marci was finally conscious enough to perceive her surroundings. Best she could tell, she was in a hospital. Machines whirred; IV pumps pumped; heart monitors beeped. She looked around. Her vision was blurred and her mind groggy. Someone was slumped in the chair beside her bed, either asleep or dead, Marci couldn't tell which. She tried her best to examine herself — was she injured? Had she been in a car accident?

The slumped-over woman must have noticed Marci's movements because she raised up, wide-eyed. "Marci, thank heavens you're awake."

Then Marci realized it was Donna. "Am I dead?"

"No," Donna smiled. "You're in the hospital. You had a severe allergic reaction last night. Don't you remember calling me?"

"No. I can't remember much of anything, to be honest." She looked around the room. "I guess it's a good thing I did call you, huh?"

A young man in a lab coat tapped on the door and walked into the room. "Ms. Ainsworth, I'm Dr. Jones. How are you feeling today?"

Marci nodded, trying her best to smile, although her lips were still swollen. "OK, I guess. What happened to me? Why exactly am I here?"

The doctor looked toward Donna. "When your sister brought you in last night, you were in full-blown anaphylactic shock. A systemic allergic reaction."

Marci tried her best to recall the event. "What caused it? What am I allergic to?"

"To be honest, we don't know. You'll need to see an allergist to determine that."

"When do you think I can go home?"

The doctor walked closer to the bed. "We'll see . . . maybe this afternoon or tomorrow morning. But one thing's for sure, I'm not letting you leave this hospital without one of those emergency self-injectable syringes of epinephrine. We can't risk you having another reaction like that again. Next time, you might not be so lucky."

Three weeks later, Marci sat on the back porch of her home drinking coffee and enjoying her view of nature. Her house was located on five acres along the west edge of town, in the rolling hills overlooking the nearby national wildlife refuge. She often spent time outdoors watching birds or butterflies, or simply soaking up the sights and sounds of nature. Marci inhaled deeply, drawing in the cool September air. She couldn't help being thankful to be alive after her terrifying allergic reaction a few weeks ago.

Marci felt in her sweater pocket for the epinephrine pen. Good. Her visit at the allergy clinic yesterday had been helpful, but still no one could promise she wouldn't have another episode. The doctors still didn't know for sure what she was allergic to. It could have been a food allergy, they told her. They had taken blood samples to send off for analysis and scheduled her for skin testing.

Just then, her chocolate lab, Buster, came around the corner of the house, tail wagging wildly. A broad smile erupted on Marci's face. "Hey Buster! There you are."

As she petted the dog, she noticed two large ticks in his ear. "Damn ticks!" she said, trying to pluck them off. "I'm tired of you guys getting on me and my dog so much lately."

As much as she didn't like killing things, she knew there was a point at which one had to use pesticides to bring down out-of-control bug populations. She went back inside to look for paperwork from the pest control company that had performed her termite inspection when she purchased the house two years ago. Perhaps they could come spray the yard.

Crawley McPherson was at work early on Tuesday, which just so happened to be the official first day of fall. He often came in early to get paperwork done before other people began showing up. The rapidly shortening days were difficult to adjust to, but Crawley loved fall, and especially the holidays. This, in spite of the fact that he was alone — no family nearby, no girlfriend, no nothing.

About 7:30 a.m., he heard Margie the office manager coming down the hall. She had a distinctive shuffling gait, which Crawley hated to hear because he knew she was probably looking for him. She was always nagging about something.

"There you are," she snapped like a drill sergeant, handing Crawley a slip of paper. "Here's a service call for you. Ms. Marci Ainsworth, 2996 Shenandoah Drive."

"What kind of service is she'a wanting?"

"General pest control. Ticks mainly, best I can tell from her phone call. But you can ask for more detail when you go out there."

Crawley looked out the window at the dried and yellowed fall vegetation. "They're not many ticks active now. Wonder which ones are bothering her."

"Well, that's for you to figure out," Margie said as she turned and walked away.

Crawley studied his desk calendar to see if he could get out to the Ainsworth property today. Just then he heard a familiar voice: MJ O'Donnell. His heart skipped a beat.

"Hey there, Crawley!" she said, entering the office. "I've been looking for you. Seems like you're never here."

"Working, MJ. Just working."

She sat down and patted the top of the desk emphatically. "I've been meaning to ask if you've considered going to the national pest control meeting with me next month. Remember me asking you about that?"

A storm of emotions suddenly swirled inside Crawley. "Uh, I don't think so, MJ."

"Why not? They've got all kinds of educational sessions. You would love it." She paused. "You understand all that technical stuff better than any of us."

"No, I can't go. Too busy," he replied.

"You're not busy and you know it," she said firmly. "Now, look at me and tell me the truth. Why won't you go?"

Crawley stood up. "I've got to go out to a new account this morning. We can talk about this here later."

MJ stood, blocking the door. "You and I have been friends for a long time, Crawley." She pierced him with her eyes. "Now tell me the truth."

He finally gathered enough courage to glance up at her. "Truth is, I've talked myself outta it."

"Why?"

His palms were suddenly sweaty. "I gotta go, MJ."

Crawley was impressed with Marci Ainsworth's place. It was certainly not like most of his accounts, which were houses carefully arranged in neighborhoods to best utilize space. This house was located by itself on the edge of town, reminding him of country houses he had seen perched at the base of mountains in East Tennessee.

She met him in the driveway and extended a hand. "Hi, I'm Marci. Thanks for coming out."

After a rush to reciprocate her handshake, Crawley felt for the pesticide cans on his service belt for reassurance. "Yes'sum. I'm here to take care of your pest problem. Where they at?"

"Well, I don't know exactly where they are. It's mainly ticks I called about. They're eating up both me and my dog and I'm tired of it."

Crawley looked around at the expansive yard. "I don't see a fence. Does your dog run free?"

"Why yes, it's not right to restrict animals. We don't own them, you know."

"Mmm. A free-ranging dog can bring ticks up to the house, you know. How many acres you got?"

"Five."

His eyes were wide behind his glasses. "I can't spray five acres, ma'am."

"I didn't ask you to spray all five acres. How much *can* you spray?"

He turned to go toward the truck. "First, we gotta find out where they're at. I've got a tick drag cloth I can pull around in the yard and try to figure out the hot spots. Then, I can spray in those spots only."

Marci smiled. "That makes sense. That way, you don't have to spray unnecessarily."

Within a few minutes, Crawley was pulling the cloth around the property. The tick drag consisted of a heavy wooden dowel with a one-meter-square piece of white corduroy cloth attached to it. The dowel held the cloth outstretched while he pulled it with a short rope. Every few steps he would stop, flip the cloth over, and look for attached ticks.

He caught nothing in the open yard, but by the edge of the trees where the forest intersected with the yard, he began noticing numerous tiny, brownish specks on the cloth which, upon closer inspection, were moving.

Crawley whipped out a hand magnifying lens and examined the tiny bugs — seed ticks! Then he fished around in his pocket for a vial of alcohol to put them in.

Back at the house, he found Marci sitting on patio furniture in the back yard. Beside her on the table was a canned drink, a bound journal and an epinephrine pen. Crawley knew about epinephrine auto-injectors because his cousin was severely allergic to peanuts and almost died one time. *Wonder what she's allergic to?*

He showed her the ticks he had collected. "Those are ticks?" She seemed surprised. "I've never seen any that small."

"Yep, first stage of ticks. People call 'em seed ticks."

"Is it unusual to encounter ticks this late in the year? I thought ticks were a warm-weather pest. It's fall."

"These are babies of the Lone Star tick," Crawley entered lecture mode. "It's the most common tick in Tennessee. The adults are reddish-brown, with long mouthparts and have a white spot on the back of the female."

"Can you get rid of them? That's all that matters to me."

"Not all of them, but we can sure reduce the population tremendously. I found some areas over by the tree line where there's lots of them."

"OK, please spray thoroughly," she said. "I'll be sitting right here on the back porch if you need anything."

"Mmm. Let me get my backpack sprayer out of the truck and I'll get started."

"Surely you can't cover much area with just a backpack sprayer."

"You'd be surprised, ma'am. It's a 5-gallon battery-powered thing. I can set the nozzle on fan spray and spot-treat those areas where I caught the baby ticks. We only spray where needed."

"Can you come back and see if they're gone?"

He stopped. "Yes, probably a week or so to re-treat if needed."

"Wonderful!"

The following Friday, Crawley sat in his office at the Peace-of-Mind headquarters eating lunch, which consisted of a honey bun and a Coke. He had finally caught up on all his accounts.

MJ appeared at his door. Crawley could instantly tell she wasn't her usual bubbly self. "Hey, Crawley." She paused awkwardly, as if wanting to say more.

He had no idea what to do or say, so he put down the soda can and wiped his mouth with a paper napkin. "Uh, you alright, MJ?"

She eased into the chair opposite his desk. He could tell she'd been crying. "No, actually not. I just found out my aunt died today."

"Uh, sorry about that. Where'd she live at?"

"Boston, where all us O'Donnells are from … other than originally from Ireland."

"Were you and her close?"

"Very." MJ wiped her eyes. "Aunt Tilly just about raised me after my mom died when I was five. She was a saint."

Crawley couldn't imagine losing his mother at that young age. Now his dad, well, that would be a different story. Again, he had no idea what to say. "Uh, they gonna have a funeral?"

As soon as he said it, he felt like an idiot. *Of course, they're going to have a funeral.*

"My uncle said he'd let me know when the memorial service is. Probably at her church middle of next week." She looked away. "I probably can't go."

MJ stood up and composed herself. She hugged him. "Thank you for listening to me, Crawley. I can always count on that." She looked at the service calendar on his desk. "Maybe we could go do a job, what do you say? That might help me get my mind off things."

"You could help me check for ticks at the Ainsworth residence. I told the woman I'd be back in a week or so to see if my spraying worked."

A weak smile appeared on her face. "Okay, let's do it."

There was no sign of Marci Ainsworth at her house. When no one answered the door, Crawley and MJ got two tick drag cloths out of the truck and headed around the back of the house.

"C'mon, we can sample anyway," Crawley said. "It don't matter if she's here or not."

MJ started down the tree line on the west side, while Crawley began by the house.

When he rounded the corner by the back porch, he heard moaning. *Where's that coming from?*

Just then, Buster ran up to him, barking and whining. The dog didn't seem angry . . . more like alarmed.

Then Crawley saw why the dog was so upset: Marci Ainsworth lay sprawled on the porch! He hollered as loud as he could for MJ, and ran and knelt beside the woman. "Ms. Ainsworth, you all right? What's wrong?"

No response, just a low moan. Crawley quickly assessed the situation. Her face was badly swollen and she seemed to have difficulty breathing. The patio furniture had a plate on it containing leftovers from breakfast — steak and eggs. He looked up at the sun. It had been several hours since breakfast. He looked back at the yard, and at Buster.

It made perfect sense. He had a pretty good idea what was going on.

MJ gasped when she rounded the corner. "What happened, Crawley?"

"It's Ms. Ainsworth. She's collapsed. Call the 911."

MJ knelt beside her, making the call. Crawley quickly searched the table and surrounding patio chairs for a purse, and not finding one, began to feel inside Ms. Ainsworth's pockets on her person.

"What in the world are you doing?" MJ said sternly when she hung up. "You shouldn't be doing that!"

"I think I know what it is, MJ." Then from a right side pants pocket he pulled out an epinephrine pen. "Aha, I knew it was somewhere around here. She's having an allergic reaction. It's gotta be the red-meat allergy."

"*Whhaat?* Red-meat what?"

There was no time to explain. "MJ, she's having symptoms of anaphylactic shock and we gotta give her this here shot."

"Shouldn't we just wait for the EMTs?"

"No, can't wait." Crawly removed the protective covers off both ends of the epinephrine pen, placed it tightly against Marci's outer thigh, and pushed the button.

MJ knelt over Marci, looking back and forth between Crawley and the unconscious woman. Marci's lips were swollen so bad they were turned inside out.

She grabbed his forearm. "I hope you know what you're doing, Crawley. You sure that'll help her?"

He stood up. "Not absolutely sure, but I think it's the right thing to do. She seems to be having anaphylactic shock and there's an injector pen in her pocket. That's gotta be it."

MJ leaned over the sick woman, stroked her forehead, and whispered a prayer in her ear.

Marci's eyes fluttered open and she gasped for air. It was labored breathing, but breathing nonetheless.

MJ sat back up. "She's breathing harder … I guess that's good."

"Let's try to put a pillow or something under her head," Crawley suggested. "That might help."

Then they heard sirens in the distance. "That's the emergency vehicles coming," MJ said. "I'm gonna call Jack. He needs to know about this."

While she did that, Crawley waited to direct the EMTs to Ms. Ainsworth.

In a few minutes, two firefighters and two EMTs surrounded Marci, putting an oxygen mask on her face, starting an IV, and assessing her vital signs. She was still mostly unconscious, but beginning to revive. A woman firefighter searched Marci's phone and called the "in case of emergency" contact number. After that, MJ tried to explain to them what had happened.

When she finished, one of the EMTs turned toward Crawley. "You administered the auto-injector?"

"Yes, sir. She seemed to be having an allergic reaction and she had the pen in her pocket. I know about that sorta thing. My cousin had real bad allergy to peanuts and me and some other family members agreed to go to the training session on how to use epi-pens."

The EMT turned and said something under his breath to one of the other first responders. That made Crawley nervous. Maybe they didn't believe him. "I think she's got the red-meat allergy."

"What do you know about red-meat allergy?" one of the firemen asked.

"I know it happens several hours after eating meat like steaks, and it's from Lone Star tick bites. And they's a lot of them ticks out here at this place, believe-you-me. That's why me and MJ was out here anyways — we've been treating her place for ticks."

MJ seemed bewildered when hearing Crawley talk about auto-injectors, anaphylactic shock, and red-meat allergy.

Presently, a cloud of dust could be seen as a second Peace-of-Mind truck made its way down the driveway.

"Here comes Jack," MJ said.

Donna's car soon followed.

The EMTs explained to Jack and Donna what had happened. They were confident Marci would be OK, but she would need to be taken to the hospital.

As the EMTs worked on strapping Marci on the stretcher to transport her to the hospital, Jack stood by, feet wide apart and arms across his chest.

Crawley figured he was angry. *He's gonna fire me for sure.*

When they loaded her into the ambulance, the main EMT turned to the group. "Donna, you can follow us to the hospital. It's the one on Chambers Drive and Tenth Avenue." Then he paused and looked at Crawley.

"I just want you to know, sir, you saved this woman's life. You got it right. That epinephrine shot was exactly what she needed. Red-meat allergy causes anaphylactic shock three to eight hours after eating meat, and its ultimate cause is tick bites."

Donna ran over and hugged Crawley. "Thank you *sooo* much. I am forever grateful to you for saving my sister."

Jack took it from there. "Yes, Miss Donna, that's why we're the best. I make sure my technicians are the best trained and knowledgeable anywhere. If you ever need any pest control services, just let —"

Donna didn't have time for a sales pitch. She turned and ran toward her car to follow the ambulance.

Crawley shook his head: Jack was taking the credit again!

CHAPTER 10

Crawley and the Out of Control Spider Problem

"Oh my gosh, Jimmy!" Jean Engel screamed, grabbing frantically at her shirt. She had been in the kitchen trying to get a griddle down from a cabinet when something fell on her. Now it was inside her shirt, somewhere on her chest.

"*Aahh!*" she screamed, trying to get her shirt off.

"What?" Her husband ran over to her. "What's wrong?"

"Spider! It's a spider!"

"Don't slap it. That'll make it bite. Here, let me help." He quickly pulled the bottom edge of her pullover shirt out of her pants and started shaking it, trying to dislodge the spider.

"Get it out! Get it *out!*" she hollered. In sheer panic, she held her arms outstretched and looked away while her husband repeatedly shook out her shirt. "Just pull the shirt off. I don't care. Get it out."

Just then, she felt a crawling sensation near her belly button. She pointed at the area. "It's down there!"

Jimmy grabbed the front side of her shirt, shaking it violently. A brown spider about the size of a quarter dropped to the floor and scurried toward the baseboard. "There it goes!" Jimmy darted after it, stomping furiously. The spider disappeared into a crack.

Jimmy turned back to his bride of just one year. "It's all right. It's gone now."

"Why did we have to move to this God-forsaken place?" Jean sobbed, then looked over at their infant daughter lying in a baby sleeper chair on the floor by the kitchen table. "I wonder if those spiders are dangerous. What if one of them gets on Molly?"

"I don't think one's gonna get on Molly," Jimmy soothed. "Did it bite you?"

"I don't think so, but let me go change my shirt and double-check."

While she left to go to the bedroom, Jimmy considered their situation. He and Jean had moved to Craven, Tenn., so he could attend graduate school at a local college. They hadn't known a baby was on the way, which now was complicating their plans in many ways. They were living on nothing but student loans and Jean's part-time work at a local supermarket, so they had been forced to rent a run-down, 60-year-old concrete block house at the edge of town. Ever since moving into the house, they had seen numerous spiders of all sizes. The place seemed totally infested. But what could they do about it now? They had signed a lease, and the landlord didn't seem too concerned. And what about baby Molly? Was she really in danger of being bitten?

"This is ridiculous," Jimmy muttered. "I'm going to call the landlord and insist he get this house sprayed."

Crawley had met MJ after work for a drink at her Uncle Kelly's pub. The small-town Tennessee atmosphere wasn't very receptive to a Boston-style pub, but her Uncle Kelly's infectious personality and persistence had managed to keep it in business for over a decade.

"You sure you don't want to drink something stronger than that, young man?" Kelly asked, eyeing Crawley. "It'll calm your nerves."

"No, uh, this here soda is fine. Thanks."

MJ laughed. "Give him a break, Kel. He's new to all this."

Crawley blushed. *If they only knew …*

After Kelly left them, MJ tried to change the subject. "Tell me about yourself. You ever go to college, Crawley?"

"I always dreamed of going to the Mississippi State University, 'cause my cousin went down there, but my folks couldn't afford no big college like that. So I started out at the local community college, but didn't get very far. Had to drop out." He nervously nudged his glasses up his nose.

"Where was your hometown?"

"Shaperville, over near Johnson City."

"The mountains …" MJ began, but stopped when she saw Crawley's wistful look.

"Yep. I miss 'em bad," he said softly. "Too flat here in the middle of the state."

"Why'd you drop out of college?"

Crawley looked away for what seemed like an eternity. "My folks got sick and I needed to take care of 'em."

"But I thought you and your dad had a bad relationship."

Long pause. "Mmm. Doesn't mean you're not s'posed to take care of 'em."

The brutal honesty silenced MJ. After a full minute, she started again. "Hey Crawley, Margie called today, giving me a new service call down in Craven."

"Oh? That's quite a way's away."

"Only about 45 minutes."

"It's a college town. How come 'em to call us? They've pest control companies there."

"Apparently it's a landlord with some family connection to Jack."

"What's the problem?"

"Spiders in a rental house. You wanna go with me? We could run down there tomorrow."

He smiled his big toothy grin. "Sure, that'll be good. I like to spray the mess outta spiders."

The next morning, Crawley and MJ made their way through miles of farms and pastureland toward the Engel place out on the south edge of Craven, Tenn. The October landscape was beautiful, and dotted with numerous mature cotton fields and patches of yellow- and red-clad trees.

When they arrived, they found the house to be a small, flat-roof concrete block structure situated in a patch of large pine trees. It was clearly run-down and in disrepair. Several inches of pine needles and other debris littered the roof, and all manner of junk, old tires and roofing material lay scattered around the yard.

Jimmy Engel met them at the front door and introduced himself. "The landlord said you'd be coming today. We definitely need pest control."

That's not all you need. Crawley's eyes roved around the property, instantly assessing all the potential insect breeding and harborage sites. He fought back the urge to start cleaning up the yard.

"The condition of this place isn't our fault," Jimmy said hastily. "We're just college students and it's all we can afford right now."

"Oh, it's fine," MJ smiled. "Everybody's got to start somewhere." She looked past him toward the front door. "What seems to be the problem?"

"Spiders. They're everywhere."

"Any idea what kind?" MJ asked.

"We need to do an inspection inside," Crawley interrupted, starting for the front door. "Can you show me where they're worsest?"

"Can't you just go ahead and spray?" Jimmy asked. "We already know they're here."

MJ grabbed for Crawley's elbow to hold him back. "We can't spray, Mr. Engel, without first doing a thorough inspection."

Jimmy's cheeks reddened, then he waved toward the door. "OK, suit yourself. Just overlook the messy house. My wife and the baby are gone to her mother's house for a few days."

Once inside, Crawley went toward the living room, where he noticed the walls were lined with old and peeling wallpaper with a faded floral pattern. It looked like something right out of the 1960s. He reached for an edge of the wallpaper next to a window and peeled it back another inch or so. He immediately noticed several molted skins of small spiders about as big as a dime. Crawley leaned over for a closer look. *Uh-oh, could it be?*

Then he turned his attention to a stack of old newspapers and magazines beside the fireplace. He began to slowly move the papers aside, looking for spiders hiding in them.

A quarter-sized brown spider scurried out of the pile and disappeared behind the curtains. Crawley eased over to the curtains and gently pulled them back. He saw a few spots of loosely spun, indistinct white webbing attached to the backside of the curtains.

Just then, two adult brown spiders dropped to the floor from the curtains and disappeared into cracks between the bricks on the hearth. When he spotted them, he knew what they resembled, at least from a distance: brown recluses!

He continued the inspection in the other rooms of the house. When he got to the bedroom, he found a bassinet positioned by an old, lumpy queen-sized mattress lying directly on the floor — no bed frame, no nothing. There was a huge mound of what looked like photocopies of science papers on the left side of the mattress. Crawley stealthily made his way around the room, looking for spiders under and behind anything he could move. He counted six more spiders behind pictures on the wall, and three hiding in the stack of science papers. One of them stood still long enough for him to see the fiddle-shaped marking on its cephalothorax, thus confirming the identification.

Just then, MJ walked into the bedroom. "Finding anything?"

He turned the question back on her. "What about you?"

"There's lots of spiders in here, that's for sure," she sighed, then looked around to make sure no one was listening. "And it's not going to be easy to treat the place with all this junk and debris everywhere." She lowered her voice. "Can you believe a baby lives here?"

When he didn't respond, MJ studied Crawley carefully. "You know something, don't you? What are they?"

"It's the brown recluses, MJ."

She raised her eyebrows. "It's a miracle nobody's been bitten, as many of them as are in here."

"They's recluses, MJ. They don't seek out people to bite."

She drilled him with her eyes. "Are you saying there's no danger to the Engels and their baby?"

He shook his head widely. "No, I ain't saying that. Brown recluse spider bites can be real serious alright. All I'm saying is that these spiders aren't all that mean and aggressive, but they'll sure enough bite if given a chance."

"What do the bites look like? Perhaps the Engels have already had bites and didn't recognize them."

"Oh, I think they'd know it. The bites usually start out as sorta a red, white and blue area on the skin, then a few days later, rot out a hole in your flesh about big as a dime. But sometimes it's as big as a pie plate."

"Oohh, that'd be bad if it was on your face."

"Sure could be a mess, all right."

"Do those nasty flesh wounds happen every time the spiders bite? I mean, is it a guaranteed thing?"

"No, not every time."

"So, what are we gonna do? We need to protect this sweet little family."

"Well, one thing's for sure, MJ," he shook his head, "we've got to emphasize to 'em that we can't prevent them brown recluse bites. We might reduce the spiders in here, maybe even get rid of 'em, but we sure can't promise nothing."

"I guess I hadn't thought of that."

"Yep, we gotta be careful here. Especially what we say to them." He paused a long time, thinking deeply. "Let's talk to the guy and set up a control plan. There are some things they're gonna have to do, like clean up this junk and clutter. Then we can set out sticky traps to both monitor the spiders and catch a bunch of them. Every single piece of furniture, every box, every container in this house is gonna have to be carefully inspected for the spiders — and maybe vacuumed out. Then me and you can put out a pyrethroid dust in cracks and tight places around the house and also spray with a good residual."

"Think it'll work?"

"Only if the landlord and them take this problem seriously, clean up the place, and stay diligent."

"Then let's go discuss it with Mr. Engel right now."

Back out in the living room, MJ and Crawley discussed in detail their findings with Jimmy, and their plan to get rid of the spider infestation. He nodded, but seemed irritated when MJ got to the part about how the Engels would need to participate in the pest control process by cleaning up the junk and clutter.

"We're busy with school and the baby and all," he said. "Frankly, it's all we can do to keep our heads above water."

"But these spiders are quite venomous," MJ asserted. "You really should do everything you can to help us get rid of them."

"Sure, we can try, but y'all are the pest controllers. Just spray the place and kill them."

"That's what I'm trying to tell you, sir," MJ said calmly. "This isn't something that spraying by itself will solve. In this current situation, I don't think the pesticide would ever come into contact with the spiders."

"This here is a two-way street," Crawley interjected. "We can't help you unless you cooperate. And, one more thing, you gotta understand that we ain't promising to get rid of 'em."

The man appeared even more agitated at that remark. "But aren't you in the business of pest control?"

"I think Mr. McPherson is only trying to emphasize that we can't absolutely guarantee that we'll kill all of the spiders," MJ said. "Therefore, we can't make any promises that no one in your family will ever get bitten."

Jimmy stood up. "OK, then, for the baby's sake we'll do what we can. Besides, my wife says she's not going to stay here with spiders like this. When can you get started?"

"We'll start out today by placing sticky traps around the house, and making some applications of insecticide dusts in the cracks and crevices," MJ explained. "We'll give you a few days to get the clutter cleaned up, and then we'll come back and treat more thoroughly. Insecticides work better if they can make contact with the spiders. And also, see if you can get the landlord to remove or repair that loose wallpaper. The spiders are living in there."

"OK, sounds good." Jimmy looked toward the kitchen. "I've got a big project due tomorrow, so I've got to go study. Y'all can just do whatever you need to do in here. I'll be at the kitchen table if you need me."

It took MJ and Crawley a full two hours to fight their way through all the junk and clutter in the small house to place 48 sticky traps and treat as many cracks and crevices as they could find. Upon leaving, they told Jimmy they would be back to check the traps and treat more thoroughly in a few days.

In the truck on the way home, Crawley was quiet. He unwrapped a honey bun and inhaled it. MJ wondered about the little dude as she drove them home. "You OK? You seem to be deep in thought."

"Spraying won't work. They ain't gonna clean that house up, MJ. I just know it." He shook his head. "Then what we gonna do?"

She looked over at him. "We're going to do our best to protect them, and that's all we can do. We'll do our very best."

"I don't know if that's enough this time," he said softly, turning to face the window.

Five days later, Crawley and MJ returned to the Engel place to check their sticky traps and make more residual insecticide applications for brown recluse spiders. Of course, this would depend on whether the family had cleaned up the clutter and junk in their house to make that possible.

Jimmy Engel ushered them into the home. After he introduced them to Jean, MJ went straight for Molly, who was lying in the baby sleeper chair in the middle of the living room floor. "Ooohh, what a cute baby," she cooed, kneeling down.

Crawley stood by awkwardly, waiting for MJ to get finished conversing with the baby. He looked around the room and his heart sank. It looked exactly like it had the last time! *They ain't done one thing we asked.*

Then he noticed MJ was examining a reddish-blue, swollen spot about the size of a dime on the baby's forehead, at the edge of the hairline. She looked up at Crawley with grave concern written all over her face. She nodded toward the baby. "C'mon, Crawley. Don't you want to come meet baby Molly?" Then she nodded again toward the baby, as if signaling him.

He guessed she really wanted him to look at the wound on the baby's head. But he didn't need to — he already knew what it was — a brown recluse spider bite!

He fought back the urge to cuss, or scream, or something. That spot might spread to be as big as a half-dollar and eat away half her face.

Jean noticed MJ's concern and knelt down beside her. "I guess you see that spot on Molly's forehead?" She smiled nervously. "We think it's just impetigo. The nurse practitioner called in a prescription that should clear it up right away."

Crawley clamped his arms tight across his chest. "Did you take that baby into the clinic and show 'em that bite?"

"Well no, we just called the nurse on the phone." Jean stood up, her face reddening. "What do you mean, 'show them the bite?'"

"You know good and well that's a brown recluse bite, as many of 'em as you got living up in here."

Tears welled up in her eyes. "You're not a doctor. You don't know that."

Jimmy stepped between Jean and Crawley. "I don't appreciate you saying things like that to my wife. You don't know anything about clinical medicine."

"Why *wouldn't* it be a brown recluse bite?" Crawley got louder. "They're everywhere in here." He waved his arm back across the room. "And you ain't done nothing we asked you to do to get prepped for the spraying —"

MJ pulled him back. "Please Crawley, we shouldn't say things like that."

Jimmy was steaming by now. "I want you both to get outta our house!" he hollered. "Right now!"

"But we came to finish the treatment for your spider problem," MJ said calmly, hoping to redeem the situation. "Don't you want us to spray?"

"Nope." He walked to the door. "We'll ask the landlord to get someone else." With that, he shooed them out and slammed the door behind them.

On the way out to the truck, MJ noticed Crawley wouldn't even look up enough to see where he was going. He just stumbled along, stunned, or crying, or both. Then she saw him retrieve a small necklace from his pocket and clutch it to his chest. She had no idea what significance that necklace held for him.

MJ stopped in front of the truck. "Stop, Crawley. I'm not getting into the truck until we talk about this."

He stood still, but wouldn't meet her eyes. He stuffed the necklace back in his pocket.

"What's that?" she pointed.

"Nothing."

MJ reached for his hand. "It's OK, Crawley, I mean, what happened here today. Please don't be mad at me for saying this, but maybe we could have handled it differently."

"Those people ain't doin' right, MJ. That baby is gonna have all kinds of problems from that bite and they don't even care."

"No, I think they do care. Maybe they're just having a hard time facing the truth. If we had been a little more diplomatic, well, maybe we could have gotten them to cooperate."

He wiped his eyes. "Nope. They wasn't gonna do nothing about them spiders."

She looked back toward the house and then at the truck. "Well, at some point we need to call Jack on this one. He's not going to be happy."

Crawley finally looked into her eyes. "They could sue us, MJ, saying we didn't protect their little baby."

She tried to affirm him. "I see now why you made such a point the other day to emphasize that we can't prevent anyone from being bitten. That was brilliant!"

He headed for the truck door. "Not brilliant, just the truth. But it might not stop 'em from suing. Shoulda' made 'em sign something saying we don't promise no one will get bit. Or … better yet, when we saw that they weren't willing to clean up the clutter, we shoulda walked away from it completely."

After that comment, MJ and Crawley made the 45-minute drive back to town in almost complete silence. They had indeed learned a hard lesson today.

CHAPTER 11

Crawley and the Rats in the Neighborhood

It was a chilly and misty November morning, typical for Tennessee. Jack Blackwell, owner of Peace-of-Mind Pest Services, tapped Crawley McPherson's image on his cell phone favorites menu, then marveled how often he had been calling that number lately.

"Heelloo?"

"Crawley, I need you go to the Robin Hood neighborhood today and talk to a man named Aaron Moyen. I'll text you his address. He's been calling, saying there's rats everywhere out there. Not just in his house — all throughout the neighborhood."

"We don't do whole neighborhoods. I don't think your license allows that."

"He's interested in purchasing a general pest service contract for his home, now go take care of him. Need I remind you of the concept of customer service?"

"No sir. I got it."

That afternoon, as Crawley was gathering his things to head out to the Moyen property, MJ O'Donnell popped in his office door. "Hey Crawley, how's it going?"

"Uh, OK, I guess. Just uh, about to go see a new customer." Talking with MJ was always difficult for him.

She leaned against the door frame. "Oh? Anything interesting?"

"Rats. Supposedly everywhere in the whole neighborhood. Jack told me to go check it out. Said the man is interested in a contract for pest service."

"Can I go with you? I'm caught up this afternoon."

"Sure, if you want to."

"Let me go get my stuff and I'll meet you at your truck. We can ride together."

On their way into the subdivision, Crawley noticed there was more than one zoning type. Commercial and residential areas were mixed — there would be a house or two, then a commercial establishment such as a restaurant, and then more houses.

"Mmm, that could be bad," he muttered.

"What?" MJ asked.

"Whenever you see food establishments mixed in with the residential areas, there's gonna be roach and rat problems." He nudged his thick glasses back up his nose. "Believe you me, I've seen it lots of times."

"How could that happen? Aren't there zoning ordinances?"

Crawley shook his head. "You never know about these crazy zoning things. It's political."

When they arrived at the address, Mr. Moyen walked out to greet them. He was an older gentleman, wearing coveralls and with hair sticking out in all directions, as if it hadn't been combed in a month. His eyes were strange — unusually wide open and almost bulging.

Since Jack had asked him to visit this man, Crawley eased out in front of MJ. He reached for the pesticide cans hanging on his service belt, as his way to gain confidence. "Hello, I'm Crawley and this here is MJ O'Donnell from Peace-of-Mind Pest Control. We're here to hopefully sign you up for pest control service and try to help with your rat problem."

"Glad you're here," Mr. Moyen replied. "We got us a bad rat problem around here. They're everywhere. I definitely need pest service."

Crawley looked around. "Inside the house or outside?"

"Oh, they're inside the house all right. I saw two last night. But they're also out here in the neighborhood, running around everywhere. Lots of 'em."

Then the man displayed a twisted smile and seemed excited, like a kid about to receive a candy bar. "Y'all wanna see 'em?" He waved his arm toward the house. "C'mon with me."

Crawley looked over at MJ. He didn't have a good feeling about this man, and certainly didn't know what he meant, but they followed him into the kitchen, where he retrieved a few slices of bread. "Now let's go out in the backyard. I've put Felix up in the utility room, so you don't have to worry about him."

"Who's Felix?"

"My dog."

"Mmm."

Outside, the layout of the Moyen house and property was typical for a middle-class Tennessee neighborhood, with rows of brick houses about 20 feet apart along both sides of a street. The backyard of each one was about a quarter of an acre in size, containing various items such as outdoor lawn furniture, clotheslines, and — in some cases, such as Mr. Moyen's — a doghouse positioned in front of a chain-link fence. Just beyond the back fence was a small ditch running behind the houses. Even though it was November, the thick vegetation was still partially green. There hadn't been a hard freeze yet.

MJ took a few photographs and scribbled in a notebook while Crawley strained his eyes, looking both ways and trying to study the features of the land. A little way up the street on the west side was a small restaurant. Even from where he was standing, Crawley could see what appeared to be a green dumpster at the back of the restaurant.

"That's not good."

"What?" MJ asked, curious.

"Watch this," the old man interrupted Crawley and MJ. He crumbled the bread and tossed it on the ground near the doghouse, about 10 feet from the back fence line. Then he held his bony arms out to the side and eased backward. "Now y'all step back. Shh, it'll just be a minute or two."

Crawley didn't know what to think. Was this man crazy? Was he calling up the rats? And worse, he seemed to be comfortable with it, as if he had done this routine many times.

Sure enough, before long, the vegetation right behind the fence began to rustle, and little noses could be seen poking out of the chain link fence. Soon, tiny creature heads and body outlines could be seen in the vegetation. *Rats! Dozens of them!*

"See 'em?" Mr. Moyen pointed in glee.

MJ attempted to photograph the rats with her phone.

"That's a lot of 'em, all right." Crawley let out a low whistle. He looked up and down the row of houses. "They's a lot of work to be done here. First of all, let me ask: Who owns that ditch?"

"I think the city."

"Mmm. Well, we need to first do an inspection, looking around outside, starting up there at that restaurant, and then working our way down here."

The old man seemed surprised. "I don't know what you'd want to be looking up there. The rats are down here."

"We absolutely have to do an inspection first, then we can come up with a plan of action." Crawley looked around. "We gotta know how far the infestation goes up and down this ditch and these houses. Then we can decide exactly what to do for your situation."

"Aren't you going to put out rat bait inside my house? That's why I called. I don't mind 'em being out here, but I don't want them inside the house."

Crawley shook his head. "It's more complicated than that. We try not to use baits until we've tried other things first. Let us look around some, then we'll come back and discuss our findings with you."

Crawley and MJ made their way up the street to the restaurant, where they found it to be a private residence converted into a small eatery. A gravel parking lot made up what apparently once was the front yard. Two cars occupied parking spots closest to the front of the restaurant.

"Wonder how they got permission to change this residence into a restaurant?" Crawley said.

"Beats me," MJ responded. "You want me to ask them?"

"Naw." Crawley turned and went behind the house/ restaurant, where he went straight for the garbage dumpster.

It was old, rusted and unkempt — and sitting directly on the ground without a concrete pad. The dirt around the dumpster was dark and slimy, as if years of garbage had soiled it. Trash and foam containers lay all around the thing, like huge ugly snowflakes.

"This is bad, isn't it, Crawley?" MJ marveled.

"'Bout as bad as it gets."

Crawley inspected the outside of the dumpster, then leaned over into it, shining a flashlight along its welded seems. In plain sight were rusted-out holes in the seams at the bottom, allowing juices and greasy gunk to ooze out onto the dirt. Then he noticed what appeared to be rodent burrows in the ground next to the dumpster.

He shook his head. "Here's a perfect set-up: Both a place to live and a place to eat within three feet of each other. That's rat heaven."

He walked to the ditch located further behind the restaurant and examined it for additional burrows. There, he had to move weeds back with his feet in order to see the ground. Before long, he spotted at least a half-dozen more holes in the soft dirt just above the water's edge.

He looked down the street toward Mr. Moyen's house, and then to MJ. "I bet them rats are living all up and down this here ditch."

As they worked their way down the ditch toward Mr. Moyen's house, Crawley and MJ saw fewer and fewer rodent burrows until they got to his back yard. There, they again spotted numerous burrows along the ditch bank.

Crawley looked over at the doghouse in the man's backyard. "He's probably throwing out food scraps for that dog. That's one thing contributing to his rat problem."

MJ walked over by the doghouse. There were large, shallow holes in the dirt in front and on the sides of the structure. "I guess the man's dog digs out these holes for a place to rest."

"Likely it's cooler down in that dirt," Crawley said. Then he pointed at a smaller hole —about the diameter of a golf ball — along the bottom edge of the dog house. "That ain't from Fido, or whatever his name is."

"Felix."

"I don't care what his name is. Them holes are from rats burrowing."

"What are we going to do?"

"Let's look around the outside of the man's house first for rodent entry points, then let's try to talk to him."

"What do you mean, *try* to talk to him?" MJ asked.

"I got a bad feeling about this situation."

Later inside, they found Mr. Moyen sitting at the kitchen table. He was sharpening a butcher knife half as big as a machete. That made Crawley nervous.

"We've finished our inspection, Mr. Moyen," MJ began. "We've got good news and bad news."

"What's the bad news?" he asked coolly.

"The rat infestation does indeed extend past your property all the way up there to that little restaurant."

"I knew they were bad, but I didn't know it went that far. What's the good news?"

"Good news is, we think we can eliminate them from your house with good exclusion methods, traps, and maybe bait stations."

That seemed to satisfy him.

"But you're gonna have to deal with that dog pen back there," Crawley popped off.

"There's nothing wrong with Felix's house," he snapped.

"Oh yes there is —"

MJ intervened, "I think he means it's unintentionally providing harborage to the rats."

The man seemed frustrated. "What about the rest of the neighborhood? What are you gonna do about that? Many of them have dogs, too."

MJ shook her head. "Not sure yet. We need to doublecheck with the state regulators to see how far away from the house we can treat if we need to. Also, we can try to talk to the city about rodent breeding along that ditch. Maybe they can do something."

"I'm telling y'all," Crawley said authoritatively, "that dumpster up at the restaurant is the main problem. A garbage dumpster is a magnet for rats and things. It's always putting out the smell of garbage. For one thing, we found that the dumpster ain't resting on a cement pad. Rats can make burrows all up under it. And it looks like the dumpster is rusted through in a few places along the bottom, allowing garbage to leak out and rats to go inside and feed. We need to convince them to ask for a new dumpster. Also, we might can get permission from the restaurant folks to let us install permanent bait stations on two sides of the dumpster, and we need to use both soft baits and block baits inside each bait station to match the various feeding behaviors of the individual rats."

MJ took her turn, trying to educate Mr. Moyen. "As for your house, you need to seal up every entry point. If your doors and windows are not professionally rodent-proofed, there's not much that traps and baits can do to protect you. You've got to examine every single place where a pipe enters your house. You can seal up those openings around the pipes with galvanized metal chase covers, sheet metal plates, mortar or cement. That'll stop them from getting inside. Then, we may need to put out rodent bait stations. Are you sure you're willing to put up with the smell from dead rodents? That might be a problem, you know."

"And you gotta quit feeding them rats," Crawley interrupted.

"I don't feed them," growled Mr. Moyen. By now, his eyes were bulging even more than usual and the veins starting to show on the sides of neck.

"You just did, when we first got here, to show me and MJ. I'm guessing you feed 'em all the time."

When the man seemed to grow more agitated, MJ intervened again. "I think what Mr. McPherson is trying to say is that we all have a role in the pest control process. We'll do our part, but you'll need to help us by doing your part to keep up good sanitation around the house — especially in the backyard — around the doghouse. Also, please only feed your dog what he'll eat. Don't let there be any excess dog food lying around. Rats will eat it."

Mr. Moyen huffed. "Seems awfully complicated. Can't you just throw out some bait around the house and kill them off?"

"No, I'm sorry it doesn't work that way," MJ said. "Rat control involves getting rid of their food and harborage, sealing up all entry points, and then strategically placing traps or rodent bait stations."

Mr. Moyen stood up from the table, butcher knife in hand. "Strategically placing traps or rodent bait stations," he repeated, mocking MJ. It was as if the man was suddenly a different person. A whole different personality.

Crawley eased over between the man and MJ. "Well, uh, we'll let you think on it. You can just let us know later if you want us to do your pest service. There'd be some paperwork you'd have to sign first." He started for the door and nodded for MJ to follow.

"But I hired y'all to do rat control inside my house," the man said loudly. His hand gripped the butcher knife handle even tighter. "You can't just leave like this."

Crawley's heart raced. "No sir, you didn't hire us yet." Sheer panic began to rise inside him. *We've got to get out of here. This man's crazy as a loon.*

"Oh yes, I did hire you to take care of these rats in my house, and by gum, that's what you're gonna do!"

He started toward MJ with the knife in hand. Crawley grabbed one of the wooden kitchen chairs and held it out toward the man. Crawley's shaking hands caused the chair to wobble in large half-circles.

"MJ, get outta here! Go get in the truck!"

MJ darted toward the kitchen door, then paused as if having second thoughts. Crawley again shoved the chair toward Mr. Moyen and tried to work his way toward the door.

The old man hollered and lunged forward. Crawley threw the chair at Mr. Moyen's feet, which tripped him. That was their chance. Crawley and MJ shot out the kitchen door into the yard and straight for their truck.

"We gotta go, quick as we can!" Crawley hollered. "He might have a gun."

Crawley and MJ dove into the truck. Crawley quickly cranked it, threw the gearshift in reverse, and floored it. Gravel and sand flew forward in a huge cloud. Soon they were back out on the main road.

MJ reached for Crawley's arm, asking in a shaky whisper, "What just happened back there? That scared me to death."

"He's a nut, I tell you. I suspected it from the beginning when he showed us how he could call the rats up."

"Should we call the police?"

"Wouldn't do no good. He didn't actually do nothing."

"But we were threatened with a knife!"

"Can't prove it. He might say we had a disagreement about the pest control contract, but that he never actually made any threats or tried to harm us."

"Then I'll call Jack and explain it to him. We're sure not going back there."

Crawley shook his head. "I shoulda known. He kept contradicting himself, saying he wanted us to treat outside the house only, then in the next breath, saying he wanted us to only treat inside."

MJ fell silent.

"What's wrong?" Crawley asked.

"I'm just glad we were together today, Crawley. If it had only been one of us, things might have turned out differently." She reached for her phone to call Jack. "We can learn from this, Crawley …"

"Yeah," Crawley snorted. "That a lot of people are just durn crazy!"

CHAPTER 12

Crawley and the Rogue PMP

Zelda Blackman heard a knock on the door. Even though she lived by herself, she wasn't scared to answer it. After all, it was 1 p.m. and she lived in a relatively safe, middle-class neighborhood. She partially opened the door and peeped her head out. "Yes?"

"Ma'am, I'm Phillip Mabry, a pest controller, and I'm going door-to-door in this neighborhood telling people about our new and exciting spray. You'll be amazed at the results."

"I'm really not interested, sorry." She attempted to close the door.

He reached out his hand. "Do you have roaches or fleas? I guarantee you'll never have them again if you let me use this new spray."

She opened the door wider and eased out on the porch, looking both ways as if to make sure the man was alone. "Oh? Never again?"

"Never again. What few bugs you have now and the rest of this winter will all be killed and won't come back next spring."

"So, how is it that you can guarantee to rid my house of roaches and fleas when other pest control companies can't?"

"Because I've got a product that nobody else can use." He grinned widely.

She figured it was too good to be true, but now he had her attention. She wanted to know more.

"What's the name of your company? Can I see some sort of identification?"

Mabry glanced up and down the street, pulled a small white card out of his wallet, and handed it to her. "Mabry's Bug Stompers. There, that card is issued by the state. You can read my credentials. It says I'm certified to purchase and apply restricted-use pesticides."

"It doesn't say that. And it doesn't show your company name on it anywhere, just your name, photo, and the words 'Category A,'" Zelda look at him evenly. "I don't understand."

"Don't have to, ma'am. Trust me, it's legit."

After studying the certification card for a minute, she had questions. "OK, so how does this work? How much will it cost for you to treat my house?"

Mabry pulled a tiny spiral-topped notebook from his shirt pocket. "First, what's your name, ma'am?"

"Zelda May Blackman."

"You own or rent this place?

"What difference does that make?"

"It's more complicated if you rent because we have to go through your landlord."

"I own the place … I mean, the bank does."

He nodded, as if pleased. "My fee is $200 cash, up front, Ms. Blackman. It's a one-time fee. I can come back and spray again for free one more time, if needed, but I guarantee that won't be necessary.

"To be honest, I have a terrible problem with cockroaches." She frowned. "Little ones, mostly in the kitchen. I've had two other pest control companies out here over the past six months, but they can't seem to get rid of them. Do you have any idea what those little roaches are?"

"No, it doesn't matter what kind they are. I can *guaran-damn-tee* you won't have any roaches after I make my treatment."

Zelda was surprised at his salty language, but she figured that had no bearing on his pest controlling abilities. "Then I agree to let you spray. When can you get started?"

"My truck's parked just down the street there. Let me get my sprayer."

"Don't I need to be gone from the house while you make the treatment?"

"Naw," he said confidently. "Won't take but a few minutes to spray around inside on the baseboards and such —" He stopped short. "But I'll need that payment before I begin."

Zelda began to have second thoughts. "Two hundred dollars. You sure this stuff works?"

"Sister, this stuff would kill a horse if I sprayed him with it."

That same day, Crawley met MJ after work for a drink at her Uncle Kelly's pub, something they had done a few times lately. They sat in a wood-paneled booth with dark green seats. Soft yellow recessed lighting made the place feel warm and inviting. Booths lined the outer walls of the establishment, while the bar itself was located in the center of the room.

"You sure you gonna drink soda again?" Uncle Kelly asked, eyeing Crawley. "We need to work you up to something stronger to calm your nerves. You seem fidgety."

"No, uh, I'll stick with Coke." He gripped the can tightly. "Thanks."

MJ laughed. "Like I've told you before, Kel. He's new to all this."

Crawley blushed. With the exception of being with MJ, he felt totally out of place.

After Kelly left them, MJ smiled at Crawley. "It's December, Crawley. You and I have been through some stuff this year, haven't we?"

He didn't know what he was supposed to say. "Uh, yes, I 'spect so."

"C'mon, relax, Crawley. We're friends. Let your hair down."

He raised his hand as if to check his hair, then caught himself. *It's just a saying, Crawley. She doesn't really mean let your hair down.*

"Tell me your most memorable case we worked this year," she prompted.

"I guess bed bugs in the chicken house. That really freaked me out, seeing thousands of bed bugs crawling across the yard. I had no idea they could disperse like that."

"For me, it was that Higginbotham case. When we saw Shea sitting in that big chair with bandages all over her, I almost busted out laughing. I've never seen anything like that in my life."

"Me too!" Crawley said. "I thought she looked like someone out of them old 1950s horror movies."

"And the look on her husband's face when you told Shea that no-see-ums don't go into people's rectums! I'll never forget that."

"I was thinking he was going to fight me."

"Me too."

"And Mrs. Welch's bird mite problem . . . Do you know why she was sleeping on the couch in the living room?"

"No."

"Because that's where her husband used to sit before he died." She paused. "Isn't that sweet?"

Crawley absolutely had no point of reference for that kind of thing. His parents' relationship had been complicated, to say the least.

"What're you going to do for Christmas?" MJ changed the subject.

"Might go to my aunt's house, but just for the day. I've got to catch up on my reading."

"What kind of reading?"

"Bug books, pest control magazines, and stuff like that."

MJ threw her head back, laughing. "You're something else, Crawley, you know that? Someone could easily write a series of articles on all of your adventures and publish them, like in a magazine."

"I guess," he fumbled for words. He seemed to never understand what she meant.

A week later, Zelda Blackman began to worry about allowing Mr. Mabry to spray her house. He had done it, all right, but way too flippantly and sloppily to suit her. She was beginning to wonder if the man had even sprayed any pesticide at all. Maybe it was just water in his sprayer.

She walked over to the wall in the kitchen to examine the baseboard. Sure enough, there was a yellowish residue along the edge of the floor, and upward about 6 inches. She bent over and sniffed the area. There was a garlic-like scent associated with the residue.

"I guess he must have sprayed *something*," she muttered. "Probably one of those organic products made from garlic, lemon peels or soybeans. I certainly wasted my money on that treatment."

Just then her cat, Beetle, entered the kitchen, salivating and wobbling as she walked. Zelda had noticed this same behavior for two days now, including twitching muscles, but today it was much worse. She knelt down and stroked the cat lovingly. "Beetle, I think it's time to take you to the doctor. Something's going on with you."

Dr. Altman, the veterinarian, had a serious look on his face after his physical exam of Beetle and drawing blood for a battery of tests. "Ms. Blackman, I'm afraid Beetle has been exposed to a chemical. She certainly displays the classic signs." He pointed to the cat's eyes. "See how constricted the pupils are? Anyway, we'll know more after I hear back from these blood tests."

"*Whhaatt?*"

"Yes, it's actually quite common among pets, resulting from either accidentally getting into something around the house, or someone purposely doing it. Does your cat go outside much?"

"Yes, I do let her outside … it's a small town, you know."

The veterinarian eyed her suspiciously. "Maybe you shouldn't do that for a while."

Zelda sniffed. "Will she die?"

"I don't think so. I gave her a vial of atropine, the antidote for an organophosphate … which seems most likely to me to be the chemical involved." He looked back and forth between

Zelda and the cat. "I'd like to keep Beetle here overnight to keep an eye on her, if that's all right with you."

"Yes, Doctor, whatever you think is best."

"And I want you to go and inspect your house, inside and out, for any potential sources."

"Like what?"

"Chemicals under the sink, automobile fluids such as antifreeze in the garage, cans that might be leaking, like old pesticide bottles."

"Yes, sir. I certainly will, but I can assure you I don't have stuff like that at my house."

The next afternoon, Zelda was resting in her living room after spending the entire morning scouring the house, garage and storage shed for any old chemical containers that might be lying around. As she suspected would be the case, she found nothing.

Her phone rang, the screen displaying the name Dr. Altman, Veterinarian. "Hello," she answered eagerly.

"Ms. Blackman, this is Dr. Altman from the vet clinic. How are you today?"

"Fine, thank you. How's Beetle? I do hope she's feeling better."

"Yes, very much so. Almost back to her old self. But if it's all right with you, I'd like to keep her one more day just to make sure there's no relapse of symptoms."

"Sure, whatever you think is best."

"Look, Ms. Blackman," he said somberly, "the reason I'm calling you is because I just got back the blood test results on Beetle and wanted to discuss that with you."

"Okay," Zelda tensed up at the seriousness of his voice. "Is it bad?"

"Yes and no. I believe information is power." He paused. "The test showed that Beetle was definitely exposed to an organophosphate, most likely a pesticide."

"But I don't have any pesticides around my house, I assure you."

"Has your house had pest control? I mean, like 30 years ago?"

"Not that I know of. I haven't been living here but six years. Why would you ask that?"

"A long time ago, exterminators regularly used malathion, chlorpyrifos, diazinon, and things like that for pest control. I've heard of people finding old bottles of the stuff in sheds or under the house. I think the pest control people sometimes gave homeowners some of the insecticide in case they needed it between sprayings."

"Wow! I never heard of such a thing."

"I guess things were different back then. Do you have a pest control company that services your home now?"

"Yes . . . well, not one company. I've had several out here over the last six months to spray for cockroaches. Three in all."

"Try to find out what products the pest companies have been spraying in your house," Dr. Altman advised. "If you have questions about the specific products, you can call me, but it would probably be better if you contact an expert, like one of those extension entomologists at the University of

Tennessee. But no matter what, please try to get this sorted out before you bring Beetle back home. We don't want her to be exposed again."

"Yes, sir, I'll get right on it."

The next day, Zelda called each of the pest control companies that had treated her house over the past six months. Each one reported that they had used cockroach baits and a variety of different pyrethroid insecticides. They all denied using an organophosphate in or around her house.

Then she attempted to call the last person she had hired to spray the house — the man from Mabry's Bug Stompers. The one who, with each passing day, seemed more and more like a charlatan. As she had feared, the phone number yielded only a recording stating that the number was no longer in service.

She hung up the phone and shook her head in anger. She remembered the distinct smell along the baseboard. "Likely only garlic," she said, hopefully. "What am I supposed to do now?"

She walked out on the front porch. What few leaves remained on the trees shivered in the December wind. The sky hung low and gray, even though it was only a little after lunch. Zelda drew her sweater close around her neck to block the chill. She had hit a wall with her search.

Then she recalled a woman at her church, Daisy Welch, who had talked on and on recently about a pest control technician in town who she said was the smartest pest man in the state of Tennessee, if not the world. Something about how he had single-handedly solved her mite problem.

Zelda whirled to go inside. "I'll get the contact information from Daisy and call him."

<hr />

A few days later, Crawley McPherson knocked on Ms. Blackman's front door. He shook his head. *What am I doing here?* That had never been adequately explained to him. All he knew was something about Daisy Welch, something about pesticide exposure, and Jack insisting he go check it out. Did this woman want Peace-of-Mind's pest service or not? Was he supposed to just look around? *For what?*

Ms. Blackman was a short woman in her early 60s, with reddish-blond hair and a pleasant smile. "You must be Crawley!" she gushed upon opening the door. "I've been eagerly awaiting your arrival."

Crawley shook her hand and smiled weakly. "Yes'sum, but I'm not sure what you need me for. We just do pest control … we ain't no consultants."

"Come on in and I'll explain everything. It's too cold to stand around out here."

Inside the house, Ms. Blackman told Crawley about the incident with her cat and her efforts to find the source. Crawley still couldn't understand what it had to do with him.

"I guess I'm not understandin' exactly what you want me to do, ma'am." He looked around. "Your house looks clean and orderly to me. And as for the pesticide issue, you can just ask your pest control people what all they've been spraying."

"I have. There's been several different companies. I've got a German cockroach problem, but they all insist they don't use organophosphates. Except I couldn't get hold of the last one, and he only sprayed one time about three weeks ago."

"One time?"

"Yes, I'm afraid he wasn't all that reputable. I never heard from him again."

"How did you come about hiring him?"

"He showed up at my door, saying he was spraying houses up and down my street. Said he had a product nobody else had, one that worked like magic."

Crawley shook his head in disbelief. "And you fell for it. Did he say what his product was?"

"No, but I'm thinking it was one of those new 'green' products."

"German cockroaches," Crawley straightened his shoulders, ready to start inspecting. "Show me where they're at."

In the kitchen, Ms. Blackman pointed out several places in the cabinets, pantry and behind appliances where she had been seeing German cockroaches over the last few months. Oddly, this time all she could find were dead ones.

Crawley carefully inspected the kitchen, puffing a flushing agent into various cracks and crevices and suspected harborages. After 30 minutes, he rose and calmly addressed Ms. Blackman.

"Best I can tell, you ain't got German cockroaches any more. I guess those pest control companies did everything right, after all."

"I can't believe it. They've been a problem since about May. Now they're gone."

He turned to leave. "I don't think you need me here any longer."

<hr />

The next morning, Crawley spent two hours trying to identify a sample of tiny wood-boring beetles MJ had collected out of a big antebellum home just outside of town. Crawley loved helping her because it gave him opportunities to be around her, but he also knew certain wood beetles infested wood over and over, leading to severe structural damage. That could be a real problem. He had to get it right.

MJ walked into the bug examination room. "Hey, Crawley! Any luck with the ID?"

He displayed a dead-serious look. "These are the real powderpost beetles, MJ. You'll need to spray."

"Ugh. I was hoping they might be false powderpost beetles, or some other, less-serious wood-infesting beetle."

Just then, Jack Blackwell entered the room. "I've been looking for you, Crawley. Don't you answer your phone?"

"It's probably in my office. I've been a' looking at these here samples."

"I want to know whatever happened with the situation out at Ms. Blackman's? The woman's house I sent you to check for possible sources of pesticide exposure."

"I went and looked. Didn't see nothing unusual. Why in the world would you want me out there anyway? She's not one of our customers."

"But she could be. You've got to always be thinking like that, Crawley — business, or at least, potential for business." He pulled up a chair and straddled it, arms resting on the chair back. "Something's going on out there. I found out today that several people on that street have reported pets getting sick. Some have died."

"That's awful!" MJ said. "What's causing it?"

"Best guess is some neighbor hates animals and doesn't want cats or dogs crossing through his yard. Probably putting out tainted meat." He paused. "It happens a lot, you know."

Crawley face suddenly turned white, and he stood up. "Uh oh."

"Are you OK, Crawley?" MJ asked.

The dots were beginning to connect in his mind. "I can't believe I didn't see it," Crawley began speaking rapidly, more like talking to himself. "But it all makes sense now. Ms. Blackman's cat. The dead roaches. The rogue pest controller. Dead animals up and down the street —"

"Slow down, Crawley," Jack said. "What're you trying to say?"

"Ms. Blackman hired a man to spray her house with what he said was a new and magic product. Said he had been hawking the product up and down that street."

"Where's he now? What's the name of his company?"

"That's just it," Crawley shook his head. "It was a crazy name like, Mabry's Bug Stompers, or something like that. The guy's disappeared. I'd bet anything he wasn't even a licensed pest management professional at all, and was using an agricultural pesticide like methyl parathion. I've read about it happening in other places, like Mississippi. It's a spray for cotton and other crops. Extremely toxic, but it'll kill the mess outta bugs. Oh, and uh, it's an organophosphate."

Jack pulled out his phone. "I've got to report this to the state pesticide regulators right now. This is serious. I bet the Environmental Protection Agency will get involved."

"I wonder what they'll do?" MJ mused.

"The regulators will probably take samples of residue from Ms. Blackman's house along the baseboards where he sprayed. If it's methyl parathion, or anything else illegal for indoor spraying, they'll prosecute the man," Jack said.

Crawley nodded. "Them men in Mississippi who were doing that illegal spraying ended up in prison."

After a long silence, Jack turned toward Crawley and looked him straight in the eye. "Crawley, I don't say this enough . . . well, maybe not at all. You amaze me, and I want to thank you for your expertise in these kinds of things. In spite of your unconventional way of doing things, I don't know what we'd do without you around here."

A huge toothy grin erupted on Crawley's face. Finally, *finally*, he heard the words he needed to hear from his boss.

CHAPTER 13

Fleas out in the Boonies

Late on Monday afternoon Jack Blackwell, owner of Peace-of-Mind Pest Services, grabbed his phone and called Crawley.

"Hello, Mr. Jack."

"Crawley, a guy named Gus Haverson called me today. He lives way out on Limestone Road and wants us to do a flea job. He says they're all over the place, inside and outside the house. I first thought about sending MJ, but since it's so far out in the boonies, it might be better if the two of you go."

"Yeah, I can do that, but you know we've had problems lately with customers not doing their part in the pest control process. This'll be another one of them, you just wait and see."

"You don't know that . . . and please don't argue. Just go take a look-see and try to help the man. I'll text you the address."

"Mmm."

Jack could feel his face flushing. "This is serious, Crawley. I want you to keep in mind that this is a *business*, and it's our customers who ultimately pay our salaries, including yours. So go check it out for me."

"Yes sir."

The next morning Crawley headed to his office to pick up more chemical for his eight o'clock appointment. He figured he could check with MJ concerning the flea job out in the country. That visit would probably require a half day. Even the closest addresses on Limestone Road were at least forty-five minutes from town. On the way inside the pest control shop, he noticed Margie, the office manager, glaring at him, obviously mad about something. He wasn't about to stop and find out why. He didn't have time today for a butt-chewing from Margie.

Soon as he got to MJ's office, he stuck his head in the door, "Hey MJ, whattcha' doing up in here?"

"Come on in, Crawley, sit down." She pointed at the chair in front of her desk. "I'm glad to see you. You doing all right?"

When he saw her studying him, he quickly looked away, hoping she couldn't see how nervous he was. "I guess I'm doin' okay." He paused. "I was wondering when you want to go out to that new customer on Limestone Road. We need to allow at least a half day for that one."

"I've been trying to work that into my schedule. No way can I go today or tomorrow. How about Thursday afternoon? You can ride with me."

"Yeah, sure, Thursday would be great." Crawley tried his best to act normal, as if there was such a thing for him. This trip would require a lot of time riding in the truck with

MJ. He nudged his glasses up his nose. *Please don't embarrass yourself, Crawley. Please.*

<hr />

About two o'clock in the afternoon on Thursday, MJ and Crawley arrived at the address on Limestone Road. Mr. Haverson's place was indeed located in the middle of nowhere. A lone white mailbox beside the main gravel road stood in stark contrast to the jungle of vines and brush along the side of the road.

"There's the mailbox," MJ pointed. "But where's the driveway? Where do I turn in?"

Crawley strained his neck. "There! They's a tiny dirt road beside mailbox. Turn in there."

"Okay, but it doesn't look wide enough for the truck."

Brush and limbs scraped the sides of the truck as they made their way down the winding driveway. After about a quarter mile, a small house appeared. It was a wooden structure about half the size of most houses with much of the white paint rotted or peeled off, leaving a grayish-brown surface. The yard looked no different from the surrounding vegetation, being knee-high in some places."

"Wow!" MJ said. "Hard to believe anyone lives here. Wonder where they get water and electricity?"

"I don't know about electricity, but I'm a guessing they got a well for water. These old houses out in the country have a well nearby, sometimes more than one."

Mr. Haverson walked out to greet them when they pulled up in the front yard. He appeared to be about sixty and was wearing rubber knee-high boots and overalls with a dingy white T-shirt under them.

"Hey there," he said cheerfully. "Ya'll must be from the pest control company."

Crawley decided to let MJ do the talking since she was so much better socially than he was. From his interactions with country folks and hillbillies during his childhood in east Tennessee, he had concluded long ago that some of them were really nice, some were a little odd, and some were just plain crazy. Oftentimes he had a hard time telling which was which.

"Yes, I'm MJ O'Donnell and this is Crawley McPherson. We're pest control technicians from Peace-of-Mind Pest Services. Our manager said you need help with a flea problem."

The old man looked around at the ground. "I'm surprised you haven't already got 'em on you. They're everywhere . . . inside and outside the house."

Crawley lifted his right leg and examined his socks and lower parts of his pants. Sure enough, there were numerous small brownish specks crawling around. Fleas!

Let's go up on the porch," Mr. Haverson waved them toward the house. "They're not so bad up there."

Crawley and MJ followed the man to the porch where the boards were warped and rotted. Crawley looked at the porch's ceiling — he could see the sky through several holes. *No wonder the floor is rotten. Wonder if it's that way inside the house?*

"Here, sit down." The man dragged two straight-back wooden chairs into the middle of the porch. Then he turned an old wooden soda bottle crate on its end and sat on it. "The wife and I don't have much company out here. Let's just set a spell . . ."

Crawley didn't have time for talk. "Are the fleas inside your house as bad as they are out here?"

He stood up, seemingly frustrated. "Yeah they are, and I guess you wanna' see inside there now."

"Well, that is why we came," Crawley said flatly. "We gotta do an inspection before we can treat for your fleas."

Mr. Haverson led them through a warped screen door that creaked loudly when they entered. From what Crawley could see, there was a kitchen, a small living room, one bedroom, and a central bathroom. On the west wall of the living room was a brick fireplace totally blackened inside and out, like a million fires had been burned in it. The floors in the house were wood, but not fancy wood floors like the rich people have. These floors looked like those inside a barn or old tool shed. A few faded rugs dotted the floors in the living room and kitchen. A small dog was curled up on one of the rugs.

"Is that your only pet?" Crawley asked.

"No, we've got five of 'em. Why you ask?"

Crawley put his hands on his hips. "That there is your flea problem. Do they run free?"

"Of course. Don't all dogs run free? They're not tied up."

MJ intervened before Crawley said anything he shouldn't. "I think Mr. McPherson means, do they go inside and out. Are they free to roam in the woods?"

"Why yes. Couldn't keep 'em in here. They're my rabbit dogs."

When Crawley noticed MJ scratching her legs, he knew it was from fleas. He checked his socks – both ankles were covered with the pests.

"Mr. Haverson, you've definitely got a flea problem. I think we've seen enough inside. Can we look at the back yard?"

"Sure, if you like."

The back yard was such a jungle that MJ and Crawley had a difficult time even determining the boundaries. Crawley placed a hand over his eyes. "Where'bouts is your property line?"

"About thirty yards straight back there. See those three big oaks in a line? It's right along there, som'wheres."

Crawley looked at his watch and then over at MJ, knowing they didn't have time to power-spray the front and back yards today. It would take an hour just to walk through all that mess in the back yard. "Mr. Haverson, we're gonna have to come back another day to do this job. It's more complicated than we thought, and I don't know if we can get to it tomorrow."

"We ain't gonna be here tomorrow anyway," Mr. Haverson said. "I gotta appointment at the VA clinic in Nashville. We'll have to spend the night. Y'all don't need me to be here to spray, do you? We don't never lock the doors. Just come anytime you want to."

"We could do the yard without you here, but we really need you to be present for the inside work. Maybe we should just come back next week. Besides, you're going to have to treat your dogs for fleas. We recommend you get some of those on-animal products from a veterinarian. So, would it be alright to come back one day next week?"

"Sure, that'll be fine."

"I could probably come do the yard tomorrow myself," MJ offered. "I don't mind."

Crawley was worried. "I'd rather you not, I can't be with you tomorrow."

She smiled. "It's okay, I can do it. Now that we've been out here once, I can easily find my way back."

"Whatever works best for ya'll," Mr. Haverson smiled widely revealing only a tooth or two. "If you come next week to do the inside, just give us a call before you come."

Back in the truck on the way home, Crawley felt compelled to warn MJ about spraying without him there. "Now MJ, I don't think it's wise for you to go out there by yourself tomorrow. I noticed there wasn't any cell service at his house. Couldn't you wait 'til I can go with you?

MJ smiled and winked at him. "I appreciate your concern and chivalry, Crawley, but I'm a big girl. If I decide to do it, it'll be fine."

"I'm asking you, please don't. There's no telling what all kinds of hazards are out there at that place."

MJ laughed it off. "Oh don't worry, I probably won't go anyway. I'm pretty busy tomorrow."

Early Friday morning, Margie met MJ as she emerged from the chemical room. "Oh good, I'm glad I caught you. The folks at that new restaurant, *Slim Pickins*, called, saying they're not ready for you to do their service yet. Something about the equipment needing to be moved. I told them I'd let you know."

MJ set down her box of pesticides and baits and straightened her blouse. "Hmm, I was just about to go out there. That guy is renovating an old restaurant that's been there for twenty years or more. They've got lots of cockroaches, and I told them they needed to pull out all that old cooking equipment so I can get behind it."

"Whatever, message delivered." Margie spun on her heels and headed back to the front office.

MJ looked at her watch. Now that she had an opening, she could go out to the Haverson place today and spray the front and back yards for fleas. That way, all she and Crawley would need to do next week is treat inside the house.

Although difficult to locate, MJ found her way to the Haverson's house a little after nine that morning and pulled around into the back yard as far as the jungle-like undergrowth would allow. When she got out of her truck, she admired the late March sun climbing high amidst a robin egg blue sky. She was particularly thankful for the sunshine this day as it quickly overcame the early morning chill. MJ grabbed her respirator and protective eye goggles, quickly mixed an emulsifiable concentrate pyrethroid insecticide into the power sprayer tank, and began unrolling the long hose to start spraying the back yard. "Always do the worst first," she said to herself, recalling that her dad used to say that whenever they worked together. To this day, she quoted it like a mantra, starting any job by doing the most difficult, the longest section, or whatever, first. That way, things would get easier as the day went on.

MJ fought and pushed aside the thick vegetation, making her way to the line of big oak trees marking Mr. Haverson's property line. "It's so thick back here that hardly any of the spray is gonna get to the ground," she muttered. She started spraying, best she could, systematically making her way back and forth at the back of the property line. The ground was totally obscured by briars and thick vines which grabbed her boots, almost tripping her. Next thing she knew, she was standing on a wooden board or panel. She swiped her foot sideways, revealing a round wooden circle. Best she could tell, it was about four feet in diameter. "Wonder what this is?"

Just then, the board popped loudly, splitting right down the middle. MJ tried to jump out of the way, sending the spray hose flying off to the side. But it was too late — she shot straight down into a dark, musty hole in the ground at least fifty feet. It was an old water well! When she finally came to rest in a wad of tree roots, MJ realized she wasn't at the bottom of the well. At least one of her feet dangled below her. Clods of dirt and mud breaking free from the roots fell further into the abyss, splashing in the water far below. She looked up and screamed for help at the top of her voice, although she knew there was no one within miles to hear her. A round hole of light shown far above. Other than a few roots protruding into the sides of the well above her, the walls were muddy and appeared slick.

MJ fought back a wave of panic. What in the world was she going to do? There was nobody anywhere around to help her and no way out. If she tried to climb out, she would surely slide back down, perhaps even deeper. She reached for her cell phone, no service. Maybe someone would come looking for her. Then, an even more disturbing realization settled in — nobody even knew she was there, and the Haversons were in Nashville until at least tomorrow.

Using her phone as a flashlight, MJ assessed her situation. She was suspended in the well shaft by an entangled mass of roots. She hoped to God they wouldn't give way. She sure didn't want to see what was at the bottom of the well. The water might be so deep down there that she would drown! Her left leg was twisted up under her, maybe broken or badly sprained. Her right leg dangled free. She fumbled around and found a thick root off to her right, grabbed it, and tried her best to adjust herself so the injured leg could be freed. Sharp pains shot up and down her back as she – by brute force of her will – untwisted her leg, letting it hang free below her like the other one. That eased the pain a little.

MJ's thoughts went to Crawley. He had warned her about hazards lurking in the tall vegetation at this place. He had even mentioned the danger of abandoned water wells. Even though she was shivering from the cold and in pain, her thoughts of the socially-off bug man somehow lifted her spirits. He was always thinking of her and watching over her. Now she prayed he would ask Margie of her whereabouts. He was the only person who might even guess where she was. Maybe he would come look for her today, otherwise she could go into shock or perhaps die from exposure before anyone showed up.

"God, please help me. Somehow, please let Crawley think to check on me today."

Doubts instantly arose in her mind. *Don't be ridiculous, MJ. You told Crawley you most likely weren't coming out here today.*

For lunch, Crawley went out to his truck to eat a honey bun and drink a Coke. That morning, he had been servicing a fast food restaurant which mostly entailed checking all the rodent bait stations outside, changing glue boards in the indoor UV light traps, and applying cockroach bait. He figured he'd make a precision perimeter treatment with a residual pesticide after he finished eating.

He looked out the truck windshield at the beautiful spring day. The sky was blue and a cool northerly breeze tickled his face beside the window. For some reason, he felt compelled to pull out of his pocket the small silver necklace his mother had given him before she died. Ever since that time, he had always carried it with him, clutching it for comfort whenever upset or afraid. In some ways it was like a good luck charm or a St. Christopher medal that religious people wore. Tears welled up in his eyes as he gingerly held the thing. At the end of the chain was a set of concentric rings, each about the size of a wedding band. He held the rings up close enough to see the writing on them. It was a Bible verse his mother often quoted, "Put on the whole armor of God that you may be able to stand against the enemy . . ." He turned the rings slowly, reading the remainder of the passage.

Crawley sighed and looked up at the sky. He wasn't sure what he believed about God, but he had seen a genuine peace and faith in his mother. She certainly had known the Creator on a personal level. Somehow, thinking of his mother reminded him of MJ. She was religious, so sweet and . . . well . . . just perfect in every way. He wondered if they could ever be a couple.

No, Crawley, don't let yourself think like that! She's way out of your league.

Just then, Crawley had a gnawing feeling in his gut. Something wasn't right. It was an inkling, no, maybe it was intuition, or perhaps just a fear. He didn't know which. All he knew for sure was he suddenly had a distinct "unsettled" feeling about MJ.

He grabbed his phone and, as much as he hated to, called Margie.

"Margie, I need to talk to MJ."

"She's not here. Haven't seen her since early this morning. Her scheduled service at *Slim Pickins* got put off until next week. Why do you ask?

"Uh oh!"

"Uh oh what?"

Crawley tapped the "end call" button. No time to explain to Margie. MJ must have gone back out to the Haverson place! Surely she wouldn't have gone back out there by herself!

He had to make sure she was okay. He immediately called her cell phone . . . no answer. Crawley left a message for her to call him back immediately, and then quickly headed toward the address.

It was about one-thirty when Crawley pulled up in the Haverson's yard. He instantly noticed fresh tire marks leading around the back of the house. His pulse increased when he spotted her truck parked in the back yard. The power sprayer hose was unrolled, leading into a dense, jungle-like thicket at the back of the yard. He jumped out of the truck, looking around frantically in all directions. Something was wrong!

"MJ!" he hollered, following the hose. "Where are you? Are you all right?"

When he fought his way through the underbrush to the end of the sprayer hose, Crawley stopped and called out for MJ again. He examined the ground, following with his eyes a flattened path where apparently MJ had walked.

Just then, he heard a faint voice calling his name. It was MJ! She was calling out to him. He searched the area where it sounded like the voice was coming from. Then he spotted a hole in the ground with a piece of broken wooden board lying across part of it.

That's an old water well! She's fallen in it!

He lay down flat on the ground and carefully crawled to the edge of the well. He didn't want to risk caving in the sides. When he stuck his head over the opening, he called down in the well for her. "MJ, it's me, Crawley. You all right!"

Now, he could clearly hear her. "Crawley! Thank God you're here! I'm trapped. Help me."

His mind ran wild with all kinds of worst-case scenarios. "Are you in water? Is it over your head?"

"No, I'm hung in some roots about half-way down."

"Okay, hold on! Don't move. You might fall further."

"Please call 911," she said.

Crawley checked his phone. No service. What was he going to do? He didn't want to leave her to drive back down the road to get cell service. *I'm not leaving her. Not even for a minute.*

A wave of anxiety swept over him. What could he do? Crawley pulled out of his pocket his mother's necklace and clutched it. *Show me what to do.*

Crawley had a thought. He stood up and examined the ground near the well's opening. It seemed firm and solid. He might could ease his truck fairly close to the well. Not too close, but maybe close enough.

"Hang on, MJ. I'll be right back."

Crawley ran back to the truck, cranked it, and drove very slowly through the brush toward the well. Fortunately, he could see MJ's power sprayer hose lying in the undergrowth and used it to guide his way. He parked the truck about twenty feet from the well's opening, leaving the motor running. Quickly he opened one of the tool cabinets in the back of his truck and retrieved his only rope. "Hopefully this thing's long enough!"

Crawley crawled under the front of the truck and securely tied the rope to one of the tow hooks. Then he carefully made his way over to the well opening, dragging the other end of the rope. "MJ, I'm gonna throw you down a rope. Hopefully it'll reach."

"Okay, I'm ready."

Just then, a thought from many years ago in Boy Scouts entered his mind. He swiftly swung the end of the rope around and made a bowline knot big enough to loop over her head and arms. Then Crawley began to lower the rope down into the well. *Please let this work.*

His heart sank after he had dropped all of the rope excess into the well and failed to hear anything from MJ. Maybe she was too far down.

"MJ, did you get it?"

No answer.

"MJ! Are you all right?"

Long silence.

"I've got the rope now!" she exclaimed.

Relief. "Okay, now put the loop over your head and your arms up through it, so it's securely under your arms. Then hold onto it tightly at your chest. That kind of knot won't slip and let the rope tighten around you. I'm going to slowly pull you up out of there."

"But you can't. I'm too heavy for you to lift me up out of here."

"Don't worry, I've got the rope tied to the truck. I'll go extremely slow, just a few inches at a time at first. Okay?"

In a few minutes, MJ signaled that she was ready to be lifted out of the well. Crawley jumped in the truck, rolled down both windows so he could hear MJ, and gently began easing the truck backward. After about a foot, he jumped out and checked with MJ.

"Is it working? Are you free of the roots?

"Yes, my left leg is hurt, but I think I'm all right other than that. Bring me on up."

Crawley hopped back inside the truck and backed up another couple of feet before checking with her again. When she gave the okay, he pulled her the rest of the way until he could see her head at the well's opening.

He darted over to help her the rest of the way out of the well. Finally, she stood up beside the well, putting most of her weight on her right leg. She held her left leg halfway flexed.

Crawley couldn't believe the sight. MJ was covered in mud and slime, hair wet and matted against her head. She appeared to have been crying. He fought an urge to hug her, but was afraid to. Luckily for him, she solved that conflict, reaching out for him with both arms outstretched. "Come here, Crawley. What a sight for sore eyes!"

MJ grabbed Crawley, hugging him and holding onto him tightly for what seemed like an eternity. "Thank you, Crawley. Thank you sooo much for coming for me. Somehow I knew you would." His heart raced. Being held by MJ O'Donnell was heaven!

After a full minute or two, she released her grip and reached out for his hands. "I prayed that you would think to check on me."

He blushed. "I hadda' inkling you were in trouble. That's why I called Margie."

MJ looked back at the well. "Whew! I'm glad you did. This situation could've been a whole lot worse. I guess the angels must have been watching over me." She smiled at Crawley, "No, I think *you're* my angel."

Crawley thought for a moment, then reached into his pocket for his mother's necklace. "Here, MJ, I want you to have this. It was my mother's and it's kept me safe from many a' dangers."

She examined the rings on the necklace and read the inscription on them. "Oh Crawley, I could never take this. It's an heirloom."

He gingerly folded her fingers over the necklace. "No, I want you to have it. There's nobody in the whole world who I would want to have this but you."

MJ hugged him again and this time kissed him on the cheek. "Crawley McPherson, you're the most wonderful man I think I've ever known."

The words pierced his very soul, soothing multitudes of hurts and rejections accumulated through his whole life. He blew out a long breath. He suddenly had a strange sense of relief. Maybe he was sorta normal after all . . .

Printed in the United States
By Bookmasters